Chrissie exte **"I'm sure you** **I came here."** *dream about* ~~seeing you in clothes~~ *again,* **she completed inwardly while her face burned with mortification. "I had to see you because I thought you should see** *these* **first..."**

Another frown drawing together his fine ebony brows, Jaul grasped the documents with an unhidden air of incomprehension. She hadn't mentioned the kiss and he was grateful for that. Time had shot them both back briefly into the past and that was all. Nothing more need be said, he was thinking, while he grasped the fact that for some peculiar reason his estranged wife had given him a pair of birth certificates.

Jaul scanned the name of the mother and went cold. "You have children?"

"And so do you."

Jaul stilled and stopped breathing. *Pregnant?* The word screamed at him. He had children, a boy and a girl. The concept was so shattering that he literally could not think for several tense seconds. The woman he was planning to divorce was the *mother* of his children. Inwardly he reeled from that revelation, instantly grasping how that devastating truth would change everything. *Everything!*

Bound by Gold

Captivated by passion

Lizzie and Chrissie Whitaker: two ordinary girls until they meet two extraordinary men.

But these men are renowned for getting what they want...whatever the cost!

Explosive passion and powerful men astound in Lynne Graham's fabulous new duet.

Read Lizzie's story in

The Billionaire's Bridal Bargain

April 2015

Lizzie refuses to marry Cesare Sabatino just so he can get his hands on her Mediterranean island inheritance. But no one says no to the formidable tycoon, and soon Lizzie is going from "I don't," to "I do!"

Read Chrissie's story in

The Sheikh's Secret Babies

May 2015

Chrissie never told her sister who the father of her twin babies was. When the Prince of Marwan storms back into her life, determined to claim his heirs, Chrissie is forced to recognize him...as her husband!

Lynne Graham

The Sheikh's Secret Babies

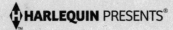

ISBN-13: 978-0-373-13336-9

The Sheikh's Secret Babies

First North American Publication 2015

Copyright © 2015 by Lynne Graham

Recycling programs
for this product may
not exist in your area.

Printed in U.S.A.

www.Harlequin.com

Lynne Graham was born in Northern Ireland and has been a keen romance reader since her teens. She is very happily married, with an understanding husband who has learned to cook since she started to write! Her five children keep her on her toes. She has a very large dog, which knocks everything over, a very small terrier, which barks a lot, and two cats. When time allows, Lynne is a keen gardener.

Books by Lynne Graham

Harlequin Presents

The Billionaire's Bridal Bargain
The Secret His Mistress Carried
The Dimitrakos Proposition
A Ring to Secure His Heir
Unlocking Her Innocence

The Legacies of Powerful Men
Ravelli's Defiant Bride
Christakis's Rebellious Wife
Zarif's Convenient Queen

A Bride for a Billionaire
A Rich Man's Whim
The Sheikh's Prize
The Billionaire's Trophy
Challenging Dante

Visit the Author Profile page at Harlequin.com for more titles.

CHAPTER ONE

KING JAUL, who had recently acceded to the throne of Marwan on the death of his father, Lut, glanced across the date-palm-filled courtyard beyond his office. A beautiful brunette was playing ball there with her niece and nephew. Her name was Zaliha. Educated, elegant and as sweet-natured as she was well-born, she would make a wonderful queen, he knew. So why hadn't he broached the subject yet? he asked himself grimly.

Marwan was a Gulf state, small but oil-rich and deeply conservative. A single king was not expected to remain single for long. Government officials had made no secret of their eagerness for him to take a bride. A royal dynasty was not seen as secure until there was another heir in the offing and Jaul was an only child, the son of a man who had been an only child.

The newspapers were full of constant speculation. He could not be seen even talking to a young woman without rousing suspicions. His wide, sensual mouth compressed, uneasy memories surfacing of the wilder and more hot-headed young male he had once been. If he was honest with himself, he knew exactly why he was being indecisive about getting married. Moreover he was well aware that beautiful though Zaliha was, there was not the smallest spark of chemistry between them. But shouldn't that be what he wanted now? A marriage shorn of the wild attraction and excitement that had once led to his downfall?

A measured knock sounded on the door heralding the arrival of Bandar, who served as the royal family's senior legal adviser.

'My apologies if I'm a little early,' the little man with the balding head said earnestly, bowing with solemn dignity.

Jaul invited him to sit down and lounged back against his desk, restless at the prospect of an in-depth discussion of some obscure piece of constitutional law, which fascinated Bandar much more than it fascinated anyone else.

'This is a very delicate matter,' Bandar informed him uneasily. 'But it is my duty as your adviser to broach it with you.'

Wondering what on earth the older man could be referring to, Jaul studied him with unsullied assurance. 'There is nothing we cannot discuss—'

'Yet this is a matter which I first raised eighteen months ago with my predecessor, Yusuf, and he instructed me never to mention it again lest I caused offence,' Bandar told him awkwardly. 'If that is the case, please accept my apologies in advance.'

Yusuf had been his father's adviser and had retired after King Lut's passing, allowing Bandar to step into his place. Jaul's fine black brows were now drawing together while a mixture of curiosity and dismay assailed him as he wondered what murky, dark secret of his father's was about to be unleashed on him. What else could this *very* delicate matter concern?

'I am not easily offended and your role is to protect

me from legal issues,' Jaul responded. 'Naturally I respect that responsibility.'

'Then I will begin,' Bandar murmured ruefully. 'Two years ago, you married a young Englishwoman and, although that fact is known to very few people, it is surely past time that that situation is dealt with in the appropriate manner.'

It took a lot to silence Jaul, whose stubborn, passionate and outspoken nature was well known within palace circles, but that little speech seriously shook him. 'But there *was* no actual marriage,' Jaul countered tautly. 'I was informed that the ceremony was illegal because I did not obtain my father's permission beforehand.'

'I'm afraid that was a case of wishful thinking on your father's part. He wished the marriage to be illegal and Yusuf did not have the courage to tell him that it *was* legal…'

Jaul had lost colour beneath his healthy olive-tinted complexion, his very dark, long-lashed eyes telegraphing his astonishment at that revelation. 'It *was* a legal marriage?' he repeated in disbelief.

'There is nothing in our constitutional law which prohibits a Marwani Crown Prince from marrying his own choice of bride. You were twenty-six years old, scarcely a teenager and that marriage still stands because you have done nothing since to sever that tie.'

Wide, strong shoulders now rigid beneath the long cream linen thobe he wore, Jaul frowned, trying to calculate the sheer immensity of the wrecking ball that had suddenly crashed into his marital plans. He was already a married man. Indeed he was *still* a married man. As he had only lived with his bride for a few weeks before parting from her, what Bandar was now telling him naturally came as a severe shock. 'I did nothing to sever the tie because I was informed that the marriage itself was illegal and, therefore, void. Like a bad contract,' he admitted.

'Unhappily that is not the case.' Bandar sighed. 'To be free of the marriage you require a divorce under UK law *and* Marwani law.'

Jaul stalked over to the window beyond which Zaliha could still be seen entertaining her niece and nephew, but he was no longer remotely conscious of that view. 'I had no suspicion of this. I should have been informed of this situation months ago—'

'As I mentioned, Yusuf was my superior and he refused to allow me to raise the subject—'

'It is three months since my father passed away,' Jaul reminded him stiffly.

'I had to ensure my facts were correct before I could raise this matter with you. I have now discovered that in spite of your separation your wife has not sought a divorce either—'

Jaul froze, his lean, darkly handsome features clenching hard. 'Please do not refer to her as my wife,' he murmured flatly.

'Should I refer to the lady concerned as your queen?' Bandar pressed with even less tact. 'Because that is what Chrissie Whitaker is, whether she knows it or not. The wife of the King of Marwan is *always* granted the status of Queen.'

Jaul snatched in a ragged breath of restraint, lean brown hands closing slowly into fists of innate aggression. He had made one serious mistake in his life and it had come back to haunt him in the worst possible way at the worst possible time. He had married a gold-digger who had deserted him the first chance she got in return for cold, hard cash.

'Naturally I respect the fact that your father did not approve of the young woman but perhaps *now*—'

'No, my father was correct in his assessment of her character. She was unsuitable to be either my wife or my queen,' Jaul acknowledged grittily, a faint flare of colour accentuating the line of his spectacular high cheekbones as he forced out the lowering admission that stung his pride. 'I was a rebellious son, Bandar… but I learnt my lesson.'

'The lessons of youth are often hard,' Bandar commented quietly, relieved that the current king was unlike his late parent, who had raged and taken umbrage at anyone who told him anything he did not want to hear.

Jaul was barely listening. In fact he was being bombarded by unwelcome memories that had escaped from the burial ground at the back of his mind where he kept such unsettling reminders firmly repressed. In his mind's eye he was seeing Chrissie walk away from him, her glorious silver-blonde hair blowing back in the breeze, her long, shapely legs fluid and graceful as a gazelle's.

But she had *always* been walking away from him, he recalled with cool cynicism. Right from the start, Chrissie had played a cool, clever, long-term game of seduction. Hot-blooded as he was and never before refused by a woman as he had been, she had challenged his ego with her much-vaunted indifference. It had taken a two-year-plus campaign for him to win her and she had only truly become his when he had surrendered and given her a wedding ring. Unsurprisingly during that long period of celibacy and frustration, Chrissie

Whitaker had become a sexual obsession whose allure Jaul had not been able to withstand.

The payback for his weakness had not been long in coming. They had had a flaming row when he'd left Oxford to fly back to Marwan without her and, extraordinarily, he had never seen her again after that day. At that point and perhaps most fortunately for him, fate had intervened to cut him free of his fixation with her. Following a serious accident, Jaul had surfaced in a hospital bed to find his father seated like a sentry beside him, his aged features heavy with grief and apprehension.

Before he had broken the bad news, King Lut had reached for his son's hand in a clumsy gesture of comfort for the first time in his life. Chrissie, Lut had then confided heavily, would *not* be coming to visit Jaul during his recovery. His marriage, Lut had declared, was illegal and Chrissie had accepted a financial pay-off as the price of forgetting that Jaul had ever figured in her life. King Lut had purchased her silence and discretion with a large sum of money that had evidently compensated her for her supposed loss of a husband while providing her with support for the future.

For a split second, Jaul recalled one of the most insane fantasies that had gripped him while he lay helpless in that hospital bed. Aware of his diplomatic immunity within the UK, he had actually dreamt about kidnapping Chrissie. Now in the present he shook his proud dark head slowly, utterly astonished at the tricks his mind had played on him while he had struggled to come to terms with the daunting fact that, not only was his wife *not* his wife, but also that given generous enough financial compensation she had no longer *wanted* to be his wife. Chrissie had been quite happy to ditch her Arab prince once she'd had the means to be rich without him. Only angry, bitter and vengeful thoughts had driven Jaul while he'd fought his injuries to get back on his feet.

'I need to know how you want this matter to be handled,' Bandar told him, shooting Jaul back to the present. 'With the assistance of our ambassador in London I have engaged the services of a highly placed legal firm to have divorce papers drawn up. After so long a separation they assure me that the divorce will be a mere formality. May I instruct the firm to make immediate contact with Chrissie Whitaker?'

'No...' Without warning, Jaul swung round, his lean bronzed features taut and forbidding. 'If she is not yet aware that we remain man and wife a third party should not be dealing with it. Informing her of that fact should be my responsibility.'

Bandar frowned, taken aback by that assurance. 'But, sir—'

'I owe her that much. After all, it was *my* father who misled her as to the legality of our marriage. Chrissie has a hot temper. I think a personal approach is more likely to lead to a speedy and successful conclusion. I will present her with the divorce papers.'

'I understand.' Bandar was nodding now, having followed his royal employer's reasoning. 'A diplomatic and discreet approach.'

'As you say,' Jaul conceded, marvelling at the tingle of the illicit thrill assailing him at the very thought of seeing Chrissie again. It felt neither diplomatic nor discreet. But then no woman had ever excited Jaul to that extent, either before or since. Of course now that he knew how mercenary and hard-hearted she was, that attraction would be absent, he reflected confidently. He was an intelligent man and no longer at the mercy of his hormones.

He had cracked down hard on that side of his nature as soon as he'd understood just how badly his libido could betray him. There had been a lesson writ large in that experience with Chrissie, a lesson Jaul had been quick to learn and put into practice. Never again would he place himself in a vulnerable position with a woman. This was the main reason he had decided to stop avoiding matrimony and take a wife as soon as possible.

His mood sobered by that acknowledgement and the impossibility of currently following through on that ambition, his lean dark features stiffened and his wide, sensual mouth curled with sudden distaste at the prospect of being forced to deal with Chrissie in a civilised manner. There was nothing remotely civilised about the way Chrissie made him feel... There never had been...

Her arms full of gifts and cards, Chrissie shouldered her way out of the front doors of the primary school where she taught the nursery class and walked to her car.

'Here, let me give you a hand...' A tall, well-built young man with brown hair and a ready smile moved to intercept her, lifting some of the presents from her arms to enable her to unlock her car. 'My word, you're popular with your class!'

'Didn't you get a load of stuff too?' Chrissie asked Danny, who taught Year Six and was in charge of games.

'Yes. Bottles of wine, designer cologne,' he proffered with amusement, flipping open her car boot so that she could pile the gifts in. 'Here in this privileged corner of middle-class London, the last day of term is like winning in a game show.'

Involuntarily, Chrissie smiled, her lovely face full of animation, turquoise-blue eyes alight with answering laughter. 'The gift-giving *has* got out of hand,' she agreed ruefully. 'The parents spend far too much money.'

Danny slammed shut the boot lid and leant back against it. 'So, what are your plans for the rest of the summer?'

'I'll be staying with my sister...doing a bit of travelling,' she confided a shade awkwardly.

'That's the sister who's married to the rich Italian?' Danny checked.

'I only have the one sibling,' Chrissie admitted, shaking her car keys in the hope he would take the hint and move out of her way.

Danny frowned. 'You know, you're only young once. Don't you ever want to take a break from your family and do something more daring on your own?'

With difficulty, Chrissie kept her smile in place. Two years earlier, she had gone down the daring route and what a disaster that had turned out to be! Now she played safe, stayed sensible and worked to eradicate the damage she had done to her relationship with her sister. She adored Lizzie, the sister five years her senior, and when Chrissie's life had gone wrong, Lizzie's disappointment, Lizzie's conviction that somehow she was responsible for the poor decisions Chrissie had made, had filled Chrissie with a guilt she had never quite managed to shake off.

'Lizzie loves you...she only wants to see you happy,' her brother-in-law, Cesare, had said to her once. 'If you would just trust her enough to tell her the whole story it would make her feel better.'

But Chrissie had never told anyone the whole story of her downfall. It had been a stupid short-sighted decision she had made and which she was still paying for. It was bad enough living with her mistakes but it would be even worse if she had to share the truth of them with others and see their opinion of her intelligence dive-bomb.

'Obviously, I'll be in Cornwall,' Danny reminded her as if she didn't already know. Everyone in the staff-room had been listening to Danny talk about his summer surfing plans for months.

'I hope you have a great time.' Chrissie eased past him to open her car door.

Danny closed his hand round her slender wrist to hold her back and looked down at her ruefully. 'I would have a better time if you agreed to come with me,' he admitted. 'Just mates, no need to lay anything else on the line. Last chance, Chrissie. Why not live a little and give it a go?'

Blue eyes flaring with pained annoyance, Chrissie jerked her wrist free. 'As I said, I've other plans—'

'Some guy did a right number on you, didn't he?' Danny remarked, his face red with discomfiture as he moved away a step and thrust his hands into his pockets. 'But all cats are not grey in the dark, Chrissie. If you still want a life, you have to reach out and take it.'

Breathing fast, Chrissie slid into the driver's seat of her car and closed the door. She *had* wanted a life, an entirely different life from the one she now had. She had dreamt of climbing the academic ranks by pursuing a doctorate and of the freedom that would be hers

once she was fully qualified. But life, Chrissie had discovered, had a habit of stabbing you in the back when
you least expected it, of forcing a sudden rethink just
when you were on the apparent brink of success. Now
she was in no position to reach out and take anything
because she had responsibilities that restricted her independence and her liberty. To her way of thinking
the most shameful aspect was that she couldn't get by
without taking advantage of her sister's generosity. Yet
it could all have been so very different, *had* she only
made the right decisions…

Long before Chrissie had met Jaul, Lizzie and Chrissie had inherited a tiny Greek island from their late
mother. Lizzie's husband, Cesare, had bought Lionos
from the sisters for a small fortune. The sale of the
island had taken place before Chrissie's twins were
even conceived and so Chrissie had opted to put the
majority of her share of the money into a trust that she
could not access until her twenty-fifth birthday. At the
time she had thought that that was a sensible idea—the
amount of money involved had made her head spin and
Chrissie had a secret fear that she might have inherited
her mother's spendthrift ways. Francesca Whitaker
had been extravagant and irresponsible with cash and
Chrissie had wanted to carefully conserve her wind-
fall for what she had assumed would be a more settled
time in her life.

Now here she was, twenty-four years of age, and for
the past year she had had to acknowledge that had she
had the ability to use that money she had put away, she
could, at least, have been financially independent. Instead, to enable her to follow a teaching career she'd

had to share her sister's nanny, Sally, to look after her own children—affording Sally's services solely on her earnings as a teacher would have been impossible.

On the other hand, by following Cesare's advice, she had made *one* good decision when she had used some of the money to purchase a two-bedroom apartment before she put the rest of it away where it couldn't be touched. Furthermore she had bought the apartment outright, which meant she could afford to run a small car and at least contribute a healthy amount towards Sally's salary. Of course to hear Lizzie tell it, Chrissie was doing Cesare and Lizzie a favour by keeping Sally gainfully employed while they were abroad. In the same way, when her sister and her brother-in-law and their children flew into London for one of their frequent visits, Chrissie moved into their town house with them and stayed until they departed again because it was more convenient for everyone that way.

Now, laden with her carrier bags of gifts and cards, Chrissie unlocked the door of her ground-floor apartment.

Sally appeared in the kitchen doorway. 'Cup of tea?' she asked, a curvy brunette with a wide smile.

'I'd love one. No night out this evening?' Chrissie teased, for Sally had a very healthy social life and was usually rushing back to Lizzie's town house to dress up.

'Not tonight…not unless I want to go into an overdraft!' she joked, pulling a face.

Chrissie set her bags down and walked into the lounge. Two babies were playing with plastic bricks in the centre of the carpet. Both had a shock of blue-black curls and eyes so dark they were almost black. Tarif dropped his brick, crowed with delight and started to crawl eagerly towards her. Soraya laughed and, rarely as energetic as her brother, she lifted her arms high to be lifted.

'Hello, my darlings,' Chrissie said warmly, her face softening as she dropped to her knees to gather up Tarif before freeing up an arm to pull his sister close.

'Mum-mum,' Soraya said solemnly, a plump little hand touching her mother's cheek gently.

Tarif tugged her hair and planted a big, sloppy kiss on her cheek, nestling as close as he could get. And all the worries and little annoyances of the day fell from Chrissie in the same moment. Her twins had owned her heart from the day of their birth. She had been so worried that she wouldn't be able to cope with two babies but Lizzie had taken her home to the town house and showed her all the basics.

'You'll muddle through…we all do,' Lizzie had assured her.

But nobody had warned Chrissie that when she looked at her children she would be overwhelmed by her love for them. While she was pregnant she had tried to think of them as Jaul's children and she had deeply resented the position he had put her in. She hadn't felt ready to be a mother and had shrunk from the challenge of becoming a single parent. But once the twins were born, she had only cared that her babies thrived and were happy.

'I took them to the park this afternoon. Tarif threw a real tantrum when I took him off the swings,' Sally confided. 'He was throwing himself about so much I had to lay him down until he got it out of his system. I was really surprised.'

'In the wrong mood, he's challenging,' Chrissie acknowledged ruefully. 'But Soraya's the exact same if you cross her. They like to test you out. They're quite volatile.'

Very much like their father, Chrissie reflected helplessly. An image of Jaul flashed into her head, long blue-black hair loose on his broad shoulders, brilliant dark eyes shimmering with anger. Hotter than hot, she thought numbly. Hot-tempered, hot-blooded, hot in bed, hot in every way there was. A snaking quiver of forbidden heat washed through her taut length. But Jaul had also been incredibly stubborn, impulsive and unpredictable.

'Are you feeling all right?' Sally asked, plucking the twins worriedly from their mother's loosened grasp. 'Sorry, you looked a bit pale and spaced out there for a moment.'

'I'm fine.' Chrissie flushed to the roots of her pale hair, scrambled up and hurried into the tiny kitchen to make the tea in Sally's place.

Sometimes the past just leapt up and smacked her in the face without warning. A memory would dart through her and time would freeze, catapulting her backwards. A stray word or a familiar smell or piece of music could rip her apart in the space of seconds, leaving her no hiding place from the backwash of old pain. If she hadn't loved Jaul, she would have got over him much more easily. But then she told herself that for the sake of her children she was glad that she had loved Jaul even if it hadn't lasted, even though he had used her and lied to her and probably cheated on her as well.

The money his father had offered her had been the bottom line, telling her everything she needed to know about the rogue male, who had told her they were married and would be together for ever. Jaul thought that money was the perfect solution to every problem, magically soothing hurt feelings and disappointed hopes. His immense wealth had provided him with a smooth escape route from all such tiresome complications. 'Together for ever' had come with a hidden qualification; 'together for ever' had only lasted until Jaul had become bored. Unhappily, it had never occurred to Chrissie when she was with him that one day she would be a tiresome complication in his life too.

'People expect me to be generous,' he had told her once.

'Just because you have it doesn't mean you have to splash it around,' Chrissie had countered. 'That's extravagant and wasteful and it looks like you're showing off.'

Jaul had sent her an outraged glance. 'I do *not* show off!'

Of course he had never had to show off to command attention. He was breathtakingly good-looking and guaranteed to turn female heads wherever he went and, if his looks didn't do it for him, his flash sports cars, phalanx of bodyguards and luxury lifestyle had made their own very effective impression.

Chrissie passed a mug of tea to Sally, who had settled the twins back on the floor to play.

'I've packed all their favourite toys and put them in my car. That'll be one less thing for you to worry about when you're packing up tomorrow,' Sally told her.

Slamming a door shut on the memories attacking her, Chrissie smiled at the brunette. 'Thanks but I've come to stay at the town house so often now that I reckon I could pack in my sleep. I can't wait to see Lizzie and the kids,' she confided.

'Max and Giana will be fascinated by the twins now they're more active,' Sally confided.

'Giana will be disgusted that they no longer stay where you put them.' Chrissie laughed, picturing her bossy little toddler niece, who treated Tarif and Soraya like large dolls and held tea parties for them. 'Or keep their hands off her toys.'

When Sally had gone, Chrissie fed the twins and put them in the bath before settling them into their cots for the night. While she read their nightly story to them, she was wondering where or indeed *if* she would have a job when the summer was over. She had only been teaching on a temporary contract, covering maternity leave, and permanent jobs were as scarce as hens' teeth. That concern still in mind, she went to bed early and slept fitfully.

The next day Chrissie got up on automatic pilot to feed and dress the twins before putting them down for their nap so that they would be fresh when they arrived with her sister and her family. She was running round tidying up, still clad in her comfortable sleep shorts and a tee, when the doorbell buzzed.

Curiosity had taken Jaul straight from the airport to the address Bandar had given him. Chrissie lived in an apartment block in an expensive residential area. His beautifully shaped mouth took on a sardonic slant. He might not have paid alimony to his estranged wife but the cash his father had given her had evidently ensured that she did not starve. Not that he would've wanted her to starve, he told himself piously, unsettled by the vengeful thoughts and raw reactions suddenly skimming through him at lightning speed. Two years ago, lying helpless in his hospital bed, when he'd thought of her turning to other men for amusement, he had burned with merciless, bitter aggression. But that time was past, he assured himself circumspectly. Now all he sought was to draw a quiet final line below the entire messy business of a marriage that should never have taken place.

Chrissie glanced through the peephole in her door and frowned. A tall dark-haired man was on the doorstep, his back turned to the door so that she couldn't see his face. She slipped on the security chain and opened the door. 'Yes?'

'Open the door,' he urged. 'It's Jaul.'

Her eyes flew wide in disbelief and she flung her head back, turquoise eyes frantically peering through the crack. She caught a glimpse of his gypsy-gold skin, a hard male jawline and then her gaze moved up to impatient dark eyes surrounded by lashes thick and dark enough to resemble eye liner and long enough to inspire feminine resentment. Unforgettable, he was unforgettable and her heart started thumping in the region of her throat, making it impossible for her to breathe or vocalise. In a flash, gut reaction took over and she snapped the front door firmly closed again, spinning round in shock to rest back against it because her legs were wobbling.

Jaul swore and hit the bell again twice in an impatient buzz.

Chrissie slid down the back of the door until she was in a heap at the foot of it and hugged her knees. It was Jaul...two years *too late*, it was Jaul. Anguish flooded her, a sharp, sharp pain of loss and grief that she had buried long ago in the need to move on and survive his betrayal. She couldn't believe that Jaul would just turn up like that, without any warning. But then he had disappeared without any warning, she reminded herself darkly.

The bell went again as though someone had a finger stuck to it and she flinched. Jaul was very impatient. She breathed in deep and slow, struggling to calm herself. What on earth was he doing here in London? How had he even found out her current address? And why would he come to see her after all this time? Had it anything to do with the fact that his father had died recently and he had inherited the throne? After his father's visit Chrissie had refused to allow herself to succumb to the morbid interest of checking out Jaul on the Internet. She had closed the door very firmly on that kind of curiosity but she had, quite accidentally in early spring, read a few lines in a newspaper about his father's sudden death.

'Chrissie...' he grated behind the door and his voice washed over her, accented and deep, unleashing a tide of memories she didn't want to relive.

She squashed those memories so fast that her head literally hurt as she sprang upright. No way was she hiding behind a door from the male who had torn her life apart!

CHAPTER TWO

CHRISSIE PEERED OUT from behind the curtain. Jaul was stationed on the pavement, his back turned to her again. Several men in dark suits, undoubtedly his protection unit, surrounded him. Her heart was still hammering so feverishly that her chest felt tight.

She had shut the door in Jaul's face, not the sort of welcome he was accustomed to receiving. He would be angry and when Jaul was angry he was dangerously unpredictable. Refusing to open the door had possibly not been her wisest move, Chrissie reasoned worriedly. As his imperious dark head began to turn she hid back behind the curtains and, second-guessing his next move, she returned to the front door and squared her slim shoulders. Loosening the chain she opened the door.

Jaul ground to a sudden halt with his hand still reaching out for the bell. Chrissie appeared in the doorway and he snatched in a ragged breath at the sight of the shorts and T-shirt that exposed every line of her long, slender legs and the sleek, pert curves of her breasts. Lashes swiftly veiling his gaze, he compressed his wide, sensual mouth. 'Chrissie...'

'What are you doing here?' Chrissie asked woodenly, inwardly amazed at how much the passage of time altered situations. Two years ago, had he finally shown up, she would have snatched him in and covered him with grateful, loving kisses. But that time was long gone. He had broken her heart, left her to sink or swim and had never once contacted her with an explanation or even an apology. That wounding silence had spoken the loudest truth of all: Jaul had never loved her, indeed could never have really cared for her in any genuine way. If he had he couldn't have walked away without once enquiring as to how she was.

'May I come in? I have to speak to you,' Jaul imparted in his rich velvety drawl.

'If you must.' Rigid-backed, Chrissie stepped aside. She was fighting not to look at him, not to personalise his appearance in any way. It was a mark of strength on her terms that she would see him again, deal with him and let him leave without any feelings whatsoever getting involved.

He was dressed much as she remembered in a soft leather jacket and jeans, casual and effortlessly elegant, his every physical movement a study of languorous grace. He stood six feet four inches in his sock soles, a fitting match for a girl of five feet nine, who liked high heels. Broad of shoulder, slim of hip, he had the long, powerful thighs of a horseman and the flat washboard stomach of a very fit and healthy male. Luxuriant blue-black hair brushed his shoulders, framing a lean-featured and wildly eye-catching face with a classic nose, high cheekbones and a shapely, sensual mouth. But it was his beautiful dark deep-set eyes that you noticed first and remembered longest, Chrissie reckoned, black as jet in some lights, bright as stars in a dark sky in others and pure tiger-gold enticement in the sun.

Something pulled taut at the apex of her thighs, leaving a melting sensation in its wake.

Chrissie only realised how much shock she was in when she saw the children's toys littering the lounge floor and realised in amazement that it had not once occurred to her that Jaul might be visiting to ask about the children. But how would he ever have found out about the twins when he had deserted her long before she'd even discovered that she was pregnant? And why would he show the slightest interest in the existence of illegitimate children by an ex-girlfriend? That was all she was now to him—an ex-girlfriend! He wouldn't *want* to know she had fallen pregnant. He wouldn't want to open up that can of worms, would he? Of course not. Her lush, full lips curled with scorn. Marwan wasn't the sort of country that would turn a comfortable blind eye to the immoral doings of its king. Of course, very possibly, his relationship with Chrissie might well fall into the forgivable 'youthful sowing of wild oats' category, she reasoned darkly.

Without a word, Chrissie bent down to scoop up the abandoned toys and toss them into the basket by the wall.

'You have children now?' Jaul prompted, watching her beautiful platinum-blonde hair slide like a veil of polished silk off her shoulder to screen her profile as she bent down. His riveted gaze rested on the gleaming curve of an upturned hip, a slender section of spine and the long, taut stretch of a svelte porcelain-pale thigh.

Slender thighs that he had parted, lain between, revelled between, night after night. He had never got enough of her. His muscles pulled taut to the point of rigidity, savage sexual heat zinging through him at speed and setting up a pounding pulse at his groin. His strong white teeth ground together, rage at his lack of control gaining on him.

Chrissie thought fast while she snatched up the last brick, grateful he couldn't see her face. It was a relief that he didn't know about the twins, a *huge* relief, she conceded, but it felt unreal for Jaul to ask whether or not she had children as though they were complete strangers.

'I've been babysitting…for a friend,' she lied as lightly as she could. 'Now, what can I help you with?'

Jaul picked up on the insolent note of that question immediately. That supposed politeness was pure honeyed Chrissie scorn and he knew it. A faint line of colour accentuated his exotic cheekbones while his dark eyes flashed as golden as the sun at midday. 'I have something to tell you that may come as a shock…'

Chrissie tilted her head to one side, eyes bright as a turquoise sea and luminous below soft brown lashes. 'I *lived* with you, Jaul. Nothing you do or say could shock me.'

Not after the way you abandoned me, but she swallowed that final assurance, too proud and too scared of losing face to risk throwing that in his teeth. But his apparent equanimity burned through her restraint like acid. It was offensive that he could approach her so casually after what he had done to her and utterly unforgivable that he should dare.

'The sooner you tell me, the sooner you can leave,' Chrissie quipped, dry-mouthed with the anger she was holding back.

Jaul breathed in deep and slow, fighting to master the stirring ache below his belt. It had simply been too long since he had had sex. He was a normal healthy male in need of release and there was nothing strange about the reality that proximity to Chrissie should awaken old familiar impulses. Somewhat soothed by that conviction, he settled grim dark eyes on her. 'I have only recently learned that our marriage was legal and that is why I am here.'

So great was Chrissie's incredulity at that news that she blinked and stumbled back against the bookcase behind her. 'But your father said it was illegal, that it had no standing in law, that—'

'My father was mistaken,' Jaul incised in a smooth tone of finality. 'My legal advisers insist that the ceremony *was* legal and, consequently, we are now in need of a divorce.'

Chrissie was deeply shaken by that announcement and her soft pink mouth opened a mere fraction of an inch. 'Oh, right,' she acknowledged while she played for time and tried to absorb the immensity of what he had just said. 'So, all this time we've been apart we've actually been legally married?'

'Yes,' Jaul conceded grudgingly.

'Well, fancy that,' Chrissie commented in apparent wonderment. 'Two years ago I was turned away from the door of the Marwani Embassy with the assurance that I was "delusional" even though our wedding ceremony took place there. Absolutely nobody was willing to see me, talk to me or even accept a letter for you…in fact I was threatened with the police if I didn't leave—'

'What on earth are you talking about? *When* were you at our embassy in London?' Jaul demanded curtly, standing straight and tall and betraying not a shade of discomfiture.

She stared at him, treacherously ensnared by his sheer physical magnetism. Her tummy flipped and a flock of butterflies broke loose inside her. Jaul had an electrifying combination of animal sex appeal, hauteur and command that stopped women dead in their tracks. So good-looking, so *very* good-looking he had grabbed her attention at first glance even though she had known he was a player and not to be trusted. Yet she had resisted him month after month until he had caught her at a vulnerable moment and then, sadly, she too had found those broad shoulders and that lying, seductive tongue irresistible.

'When, Chrissie?' he repeated doggedly.

'Oh, a little while after my *imaginary* husband disappeared into thin air,' Chrissie supplied. 'And then shortly after my final visit to the embassy, your father came to see me and explained and everything became clear.'

'I don't know what you hope to achieve by talking nonsense like this at a point when all either of us can want is a divorce.'

Chrissie elevated a very fine brow. 'I don't know, Jaul…do you think it could be anger motivating me after what you put me through?'

'Anger has no place here. We have lived apart for a long time. I want a divorce. This is a practical issue, nothing more,' Jaul delivered crushingly.

'You do know that I hate you?' Chrissie pressed shakily, a flicker of hysteria firing her that he could stand there evidently untouched as though nothing of any great import had ever happened between them. Yet once he had pursued her relentlessly and had sworn that he *loved* her and that only the security of marriage would satisfy him. There was nothing deader than an old love affair, a little voice cried plaintively inside her, and the proof of that old maxim stood in front of her.

Jaul was thinking of the woman who had left him lying unvisited in his hospital bed and he met her angry gaze with coldly contemptuous dark eyes. 'Why would I care?'

He didn't feel like Jaul any more; he had changed out of all recognition, Chrissie acknowledged numbly. He wanted a divorce; he *needed* a divorce. But she was still struggling to get her head around the astonishing fact that they had genuinely been married for over two years. 'Why did your father tell me that our marriage was illegal?'

His lean, strong face tautened. 'It was not a lie. He believed it to be illegal—'

'But that's not all he believed,' Chrissie whispered. 'He told me that you'd deliberately gone through that ceremony with me *knowing* it was illegal and that you could wriggle out of the commitment and walk away any time you wanted—'

'I refuse to believe that he would ever have said or even implied anything of that nature,' Jaul derided with an emphatic shake of his imperious dark head. 'He was an honourable man and a caring father—'

'Like hell he was!' Chrissie slammed back at him in sudden fury, goaded by that provocative statement into losing all self-control. 'I was thrown out of your apartment wearing only the clothes I was standing up in. I was treated like an illegal squatter and absolutely humiliated—'

'These grossly disrespectful lies gain you no ground with me. I will not listen to them,' Jaul spelt out, his beautiful, wilful mouth twisting. 'I know you for the woman you are. My father gave you five million pounds to get out of my life and you took it and I never heard from you again—'

'Well, admittedly I didn't get very far at the Marwani Embassy where women claiming to be your wife, illegal or otherwise, are treated like lunatics,' Chrissie parried flatly, declining to answer that accusation about the bank draft she had refused to use because it seemed Jaul wasn't prepared to listen or believe anything she said in her own defence.

Chrissie could never have accepted that hateful 'blood' money, intended to buy her discretion and silence and dissuade her from approaching the media to sell some sleazy story about her experiences with Jaul.

Jaul set his even white teeth together. 'I want you to leave the past where it belongs and concentrate on the important issue here...our *divorce*.'

Without warning, Chrissie's eyes sparkled like gold-dusted turquoises. 'You want a divorce to remarry, don't you?'

'Why I want it scarcely matters this long after the event,' Jaul fielded drily.

'You need my consent to get a divorce,' Chrissie assumed, walking past him back to the front door, thinking that this time around the ball was in her court and the power hers. Jaul expected her to be understanding and helpful and give him what he wanted. But why *should* she be understanding? She owed him nothing!

'Naturally...if it is to go through fast it has to be uncontested—'

'The answer is no,' Chrissie delivered, far from being in a cooperative frame of mind. She was bitter about the way he had treated her and stubbornly ready to make things difficult for him. 'If we're truly married and you now want a divorce, you'll have to *fight* me for it.'

Jaul stilled in the lounge doorway, dark eyes flashing bright as a flame. 'But that's ridiculous…why would you do something that stupid?'

'Because I can,' Chrissie replied, truthful to the last word. 'I won't willingly do anything which suits you and I know you want to keep all this on the down-low. After all, you never did own up publicly to the shame of marrying a foreigner, did you?'

'I believed the marriage was invalid!' Jaul shot back at her, lean brown hands coiling into fists. 'Why would I have talked about it?'

'Well, most guys would at least have talked about it to the woman who believed she was married to them,' Chrissie pointed out scornfully as she stretched out a hand to open the door. 'But you…what did you do? Oh, yes…you ran out on me and left your daddy to clear up the mess you left behind you!'

Sheer rage at that unjust condemnation engulfed Jaul so fast he was dizzy with it. He snapped long fingers round a slender wrist before she could open the door. Smouldering dark golden eyes raked her flushed and defiant face. 'You will *not* speak to me like that.'

Suppressing a spasm of dismay, Chrissie forced herself to laugh and her eyes sparkled with challenge. 'Message to Jaul—I can speak to you any way I like and there's not a darned thing you can do about it! You don't deserve anything better from me after the way you treated me…'

With a contemptuous flick of his long fingers, Jaul

relinquished his hold on her. Dark eyes still sparking like high-voltage wires, he scanned her with derision. 'Is this your way of trying to push the price up? You want me to *pay* you to set me free from this marriage?'

A genuine laugh fell from Chrissie's taut mouth. 'Oh, no, I've got plenty of money,' she told him blithely. 'I don't want a penny from you. I only want to make you sweat.'

Jaul no longer trusted his temper or his control. Nobody had spoken to him like that since he had last seen Chrissie and it was a salutary lesson. Their personalities had been on a collision course from day one. Both of them were strong-willed, obstinate and quick-tempered. They had had monumental fights and even more shattering reconciliations. In fact those reconciliations had been such sweet fantasies Jaul had never forgotten them and he got hot and hard even thinking about them, a recollection as unwelcome as it was dangerous.

His beautifully shaped mouth flattening the sultry curl tugging at the edges, fine ebony brows drawing together in a frown of censure, he breathed curtly, 'I can see there's no talking to you in the mood you're in—'

'I'm *not* in a mood!' Chrissie proclaimed furiously, catching an involuntary snatch of the spicy cologne he wore, her senses reeling at the sudden flood of familiarity that made her ache and hurt as if his betrayal were as recent as yesterday. It also reminded her of hot, sweaty nights and incredible passion, a thought which instantly infuriated her.

'I'll return later when you've had time to think over what I've told you,' he informed her with typical tenacity.

Chrissie bit back the admission that she would be staying at her sister's home for several days. That was her business, not his, and she had no intention of telling him anything likely to lead to his discovery that he was not only married but also a father. That would be setting the cat among the pigeons with a vengeance, she conceded worriedly, and it was not something she was prepared to risk without knowing where she stood.

The strained silence smouldered.

'A divorce is the only sensible option and I don't object to paying for the privilege,' Jaul grated between clenched teeth, out of all patience with her reluctance to discuss the issue. 'As my wife, estranged or otherwise, you're naturally entitled to my financial support—'

'I want nothing from you,' Chrissie repeated doggedly. 'Please leave.'

Long bronzed fingers bit into the edge of the door as Jaul fought a powerful impulse to say something, *anything*, that would stir her into a more natural reaction. What had happened to his bright and fearless Chrissie? He glanced at her in frustration. Her eyes were blank, her delicately pointed features empty of expression. Her entire attitude spelt out the message that he was the enemy and not to be trusted.

Without another word, Jaul walked out of the building, determined that he would not see her again. He had told her what he had to tell her. And now he would step back and let the lawyers handle the rest of it.

Chrissie got dressed in a feverish surge of activity. She flung clothes into a small case, carrying it and other pieces of baby paraphernalia out to the car. Her home had always been her sanctuary but now it felt violated by Jaul's visit and she no longer felt safe there. What if he had walked in and the twins had been present? Why did she imagine that he would have instantly recognised his own children when he had no reason to even suspect their existence? She was being hysterical and foolish, she told herself shamefacedly, but even so she could barely wait to get Tarif and Soraya strapped into their car seats and drive away from the apartment.

As she drove through the busy mid-morning traffic she had too much time to look back into the past. Memories she didn't want bombarded her. Indeed she could never think about her years at university without thinking of Jaul because he had always been there on the outskirts of her life, long unacknowledged but always noticed and never forgotten.

She had shared a tiny flat with another girl when in her second year at university. Nessa had been just a little man-mad, to the extent that Chrissie had tended to switch off when Nessa began talking about her latest lover. But even Nessa had gone into thrilled overdrive when she'd first met a prince. Chrissie had been less impressed, well aware that in some Eastern countries princes were ten a penny and not much more important. Jaul, however, had proved somewhat harder to overlook. He had flown Nessa to Paris in his private jet just for dinner and Nessa had been incoherent with excitement at the luxury of the experience.

Jaul had brought Nessa home the next day and had been in the flat when Chrissie had come home from the classes that her roommate had skipped. Chrissie still remembered her first glimpse of Jaul, his gypsy-dark skin and eyes brilliant as newly minted gold in sunlight, his lean, breathtakingly handsome face intent.

He had stared at Chrissie for the longest time and she hadn't been able to breathe or look away while Nessa gabbled incoherently about Paris and limousines. Jaul had taken his leave quickly.

'He was amazing in bed,' Nessa had confided as soon as he was gone, languorously rolling her eyes and quite uninhibited about admitting that she had slept with Jaul on the first date. 'Absolutely freakin' *amazing!*'

But for all that it had still been a one-night stand. Jaul had followed up by having flowers and a very pretty pair of diamond earrings delivered to Nessa, but he hadn't phoned again. Nessa had been disappointed but accepting, pointing out that, with all Jaul had to offer, he was sure to want to make the most of his freedom.

The next time Chrissie had seen Jaul she had been in the student union. She had noticed Jaul, naturally. She could scarcely have failed to notice his presence when he was surrounded by a quartet of suited sunglasses-wearing bodyguards and a crowd of giggling flirtatious blondes who, as she soon learnt, seemed to appear out of nowhere to engulf him wherever he went.

He had startled her by springing upright as she was passing his table and had insisted on acknowledging her when she would've passed on by without a word. Stiff with discomfiture, Chrissie had been cool, inordinately aware of the heat in his dark gaze and the jealous scrutiny of his female companions.

Back then Chrissie had been working two part-time jobs to survive at university because her family could not afford to help her out. One of Chrissie's jobs during term time had been stacking shelves in the library, the other waitressing at a local restaurant, but she had still found it a major challenge to meet her bills. Her father had still been a tenant farmer, whose ill-health had forced him into retirement while her older sister, Lizzie, had worked night and day to keep the farm going, while Chrissie continued her studies, but the knowledge that, without her, her family was having an even tougher struggle to survive had filled her with guilt.

But even as a child Chrissie had recognised that her late mother Francesca's chaotic life might have been less dysfunctional had she had a career to fall back on when her affairs with unsuitable men fell apart. A woman needed more than a basic education to survive and Chrissie had always been determined to build her life round a career rather than a man. Her mother's marriage to her father had been short-lived and the relationships that Francesca had got involved in afterwards had been destructive ones in which alcohol, infidelity, physical violence and other evils had prevailed. Shorn of her innocence at a very young age, Chrissie knew just how low a woman could be forced to sink to keep food on the table and it was a lesson she would never forget. No, Chrissie would never willingly put herself in a position where she had to depend on a man to keep her.

When Jaul had approached her in the library where she was stacking shelves one day a few weeks after their first meeting to ask for her help in finding a book, she had been polite and helpful as befitted a humble employee keen to keep her job.

'I'd like to take you out to dinner some evening,' he had murmured after she'd slotted the book into his lean brown hand.

He had the most stunning dark eyes, pure lustrous

jet enticement in his lean, darkly handsome face. In his presence her mouth had run dry and her breathing had fractured while she'd marvelled at the weird way she'd kept on wanting to look at him, an urge so powerful it had almost qualified as a *need*. Infuriated by the dizzy way she was reacting, she'd thought instead of how he had treated Nessa. Jaul had chased sexual conquest, nothing more complex. Once the chase was over and he had got what he wanted he'd lost interest and casual sex with young women as uninhibited and adventurous as Nessa had suited him perfectly. He hadn't been looking for a relationship with all the limits that would have involved. He hadn't been offering friendship or caring or fidelity.

'I'm sorry, no,' Chrissie had said woodenly.

'Why not?' Jaul had asked without hesitation.

'Between my studies and my two part-time jobs, I have very little free time,' Chrissie had told him. 'And when I do have it, I tend to go home and visit my family.'

'Lunch, then,' Jaul had suggested smoothly. 'Surely you could lunch with me some day?'

'But I don't want to,' Chrissie had confessed abruptly, backing off a step, feeling cornered and slightly intimidated by the sheer height and size of him in the narrow space between the book stacks.

A fine ebony brow had quirked. 'I have offended you in some way?'

'We just wouldn't suit,' Chrissie had countered between gritted teeth, her irritation rising at his refusal to simply accept her negative response.

'In what way?'

'You're everything I don't like,' Chrissie had framed

in a sudden burst of frustration. 'You don't study, you party. You run around with a lot of different women. I'm not your type. I don't want to go to Paris for dinner! I don't want diamonds! I haven't the slightest intention of going to bed with you!'

'And if I didn't offer you Paris, diamonds or sex?'

'I'd probably end up trying to kill you because you're so blasted full of yourself!' Chrissie had shot at him in a rage. 'Why can't you just take no for an answer?'

Jaul had suddenly grinned, a shockingly charismatic grin that had made her tummy somersault. 'I wasn't brought up to take no for an answer.'

'With me, no *means* no!' Chrissie had told him angrily. 'Persistence only annoys me—'

'And I am very persistent as well as full of myself,' Jaul had acknowledged softly. 'It seems we are at an impasse—'

Chrissie had stabbed a finger to indicate the directional arrow pointing down to the nearest study area. 'You have your book—go study.'

And without another word she had walked away with her trolley, heading for the lift that would let her escape to the floor above.

CHAPTER THREE

CARRYING A TWIN in each arm, Chrissie was greeted by Sally at the front door of Cesare and Lizzie's home. Her nephew and niece, Max and Giana, clustered round the two women eager to see their cousins. Tarif whooped with excitement when he saw Max and opened his arms to the older boy.

'He *knows* me!' Max carolled in amazement.

'Once Tarif's walking, he'll plague the life out of you,' Chrissie quipped, passing over Tarif while Sally took charge of Soraya because Giana was too young to manage her.

An elegant and visibly pregnant blonde with green eyes and a ready smile came out of one of the rooms leading off the spacious hall. 'Chrissie...*lovely*. I wasn't expecting you until later,' Lizzie confided warmly.

The tears still burning behind Chrissie's eyes suddenly spilled over without warning. As she saw her big sister look at her in astonishment Chrissie swallowed back a sob and blundered into her sibling's outspread arms. *'Sorry.'*

'You don't need to apologise if something's upset you,' Lizzie insisted. 'What on earth has happened? You never cry—'

Fortunately Lizzie had not been exposed to Chrissie's grief two years earlier once it had finally dawned on her that Jaul was not returning to the UK. It had been a matter of pride to Chrissie that she should not distress her otherwise happy sister with the sad tale of how she had screwed up her own life. She had put a brave face on her abandonment and subsequent pregnancy, talking lightly and always unemotionally of a relationship that had broken down and a young man unwilling to acknowledge responsibility for the babies she'd carried.

'You don't need the creep…you don't need anyone but Cesare and me!' Lizzie had told her comfortingly and she had asked no further questions.

Now as Chrissie bit back the sobs clogging her throat she was faced with the reality that as she had never told her sister about Jaul, she had to do it now. Emotional turmoil had been building up inside her from the very moment Jaul had appeared at her front door. Her past had pierced the present and most painfully, for all the gloriously happy and agonisingly sad memories of Jaul she had packed away were now flooding through the gap in her defences and hurting her all over again.

'For goodness' sake,' Lizzie exclaimed, banding an arm round her taller sister to urge her into the drawing room with its comfortable blue sofas and sleek pale contemporary furniture.

Cesare was talking on his mobile by the window and he concluded the call, frowning with concern when he registered the tear-stained distress stamped on his sister-in-law's face.

'I was just about to tell you that my sisters are arriv-

ing this evening and expecting you to go out clubbing
with them tomorrow night—'

Chrissie tried to force a smile because she got on
like a house on fire with Cesare's younger sisters, Sofia
and Maurizia, and the three women always went out together when they visited London. 'I might not be good
company—'

Lizzie pressed her gently down onto a sofa. 'Tell me
what's wrong—'

Chrissie groaned. 'I *can't*. I've been such an idiot
otherwise I would've told you years ago. You won't
believe how stupid I've been and now I don't know
what to do—'

'Starting at the beginning usually helps,' Cesare incised.

'The twins' father has turned up,' Chrissie revealed
tautly. 'And he says we need a divorce, which doesn't
make sense after what his father—'

Cesare stopped dead to skim her an incredulous
glance. 'You were *married* to the twins' father?'

'My goodness, I certainly didn't see that coming!
Married!' Lizzie admitted in shock, sinking down on
an ottoman near her sister. Chrissie felt guiltier than
ever, looking back over the years to acknowledge that
Lizzie had been a better mother to her than their own
mother, even though Lizzie was only five years older
than Chrissie.

'Right, the beginning,' Chrissie reminded herself in
receipt of a wry appraisal from Cesare. 'Or you won't
know what I'm talking about.'

And Chrissie tried with some difficulty to put into
words how long she had known Jaul without ever getting to know him properly.

'But you never ever mentioned him,' Lizzie commented in a continuing tone of disbelief. 'You knew him all the time you were at uni and yet you never told me about him!'

Chrissie reddened fiercely, quite unable to describe how much of a silent role Jaul had played in her life long before she'd ever actually got involved with him. She had seen him on campus most days, occasionally speaking to him, occasionally avoiding him if he had been more than usually keen to press his interest in her. What she had never ever contrived to be with Jaul was indifferent. When he wasn't there, she had found herself looking for him. If a couple of days had gone by without a glimpse of him, she would be like someone starved of food and craving it and when he had reappeared she would study him with helpless intensity as if looking alone could revive her energies.

In many ways Jaul had been her most secret and private fantasy. She could never ever have explained their relationship to her sister without feeling mortified and she had been even more grateful that she had kept him quiet when, instead of getting to bring Jaul home to show him off along with her wedding ring, she had ended up coming home dumped and pregnant. Lizzie had been very hurt on Chrissie's behalf when their father had said he didn't want his unmarried pregnant daughter to visit, but Chrissie had felt much guiltier about upsetting and disappointing the sister she had always idolised, the big sister who had made so many sacrifices on her behalf. Having left school at sixteen to work on their father's farm, Lizzie had never got a further education or the chance to be young and care-free for even a few years.

'There was no need to mention Jaul. It was only during our last year at uni that we actually got involved,' Chrissie pointed out ruefully.

'And yet you *still* didn't mention him,' Cesare reminded her drily.

'I honestly assumed we wouldn't last. I thought we would be over and done again in five minutes. It was all so unexpected. I didn't think Jaul *did* serious and then everything somehow changed and I changed too… that's the only way I can describe it,' she mumbled uncomfortably.

'You fell in love with him,' Lizzie interpreted.

'Truly, madly and deeply and all that,' Chrissie joked heavily. 'We got married at the Marwani Embassy here and we had a civil ceremony as well.'

'But why such secrecy?' Cesare enquired.

'Jaul didn't want anyone knowing we had got married until he had had the chance to tell his father about us…which I don't think he was in any hurry to do.' Chrissie hesitated and then mentioned the argument that had taken place when a few weeks after the wedding Jaul had announced his intention of returning to Marwan alone without any reference to when he planned to return. 'I felt rejected.'

'Of course you did,' Lizzie said warmly, squeezing Chrissie's hand gently.

Chrissie told them about her fruitless visits to the Marwani Embassy and then the visit from Jaul's father, King Lut, that had followed. When she then repeated what the older man had told her, Cesare became undeniably angry.

'That was when you should've come to us for support and advice!'

'I still thought Jaul would come back to me. I didn't instantly accept everything that his father told me and I hadn't given up hope.'

'And then you discovered that you were pregnant,' Lizzie guessed.

'A couple of months had passed by then and I couldn't excuse Jaul's silence any longer. I realised that his father must have been telling me the truth.'

'But evidently he wasn't,' Cesare cut in, already thinking ahead. 'Does Jaul know about the twins?'

'No. I didn't tell him. And I told him I wouldn't give him a divorce just to annoy him,' Chrissie confided uncomfortably. 'That was pretty childish of me, wasn't it?'

'I'll put my lawyers on this,' Cesare informed her, compressing his well-shaped mouth. 'Jaul needs to be told about the twins asap. A man has the right to know his own children—'

'Even if he deserts his wife and never gets back in touch?' Lizzie protested emotively.

'*Sì*, even then,' Cesare murmured ruefully.

Chrissie told Cesare and Lizzie about her repeated visits to the Marwani Embassy and her continued and equally fruitless attempts to contact Jaul by phone. 'So, you see, I did try very hard to track him down.'

'But you still need to take a long-term view of this situation, Chrissie. Set aside the hostility. Concentrate on the children and the future and you won't go far wrong.'

'And you do owe Jaul *one* favour,' Lizzie said ruefully, startling Chrissie, who was dabbing her face dry and grateful the tear overflow had run its course. 'You have to go and see him and tell him about the twins before you bring in the lawyers—'

'For goodness' sake, I don't even know where he's staying!' Chrissie parried, aghast at that suggestion. 'In fact he might only have been passing through London.'

'Why does Chrissie owe Jaul another meeting?' Cesare enquired of his wife, equally in the dark on that score.

'He at least had the decency to tell her that they were still married himself, rather than from his lawyers,' Lizzie pointed out.' I don't think you owe him anything more, Chrissie, but I do think he deserves the chance to learn that he's a father from you and nobody else and in private.'

'I don't want to see him…don't even know if he's still here in London… I've got nothing to wear either!' Chrissie argued in an unashamed surge of protest, but behind it she knew she was caught because, like her older sister, she also had a sense of fair play.

Jaul had not been comfortable visiting her but, even so, he had done it because he knew it was the right thing to do. How could she be seen to do less?

Chrissie climbed out of the taxi that Lizzie had insisted she needed, pointing out that searching for a parking space while trying to identify the correct house was the last thing her sister needed in the mood she was in.

Not that finding the house where Jaul was staying had proved a problem, Chrissie acknowledged ruefully, shooting the vast monolith of a building in the most exclusive part of London a wry glance. Cesare's staff had come up with all the required information. With the kind of high-powered connections her brother-in-law enjoyed, tracking down Jaul had not proved that big a challenge while it had also provided her with extrane-

ous information she had not required. For instance, the
huge town house had formerly been an entire crescent
of smaller dwellings and it had been purchased in the
nineteen thirties and turned into a single dwelling by
Jaul's grandfather to house the Marwani royal family
and their numerous staff whenever they came to visit
London. Apparently the family had made ridiculously
few visits in the many years that had passed since then.

It had been an education for Chrissie to discover that
this was one more fact she hadn't known about the man
she had loved and married. Although they had visited
London together, he had never once mentioned that his
family owned a house there. In much the same way he
had never mentioned that he was an only child des-
tined to become a king. His Marwani background had
always been a closed book to her from which he had
offered her a glimpse of very few pages. In short she
knew he had grown up without a mother, had attended
a military school and had trained as a soldier in Saudi
Arabia. When he'd signed up to study politics at Oxford
University it had been his very first visit to the UK.

It shook Chrissie now to accept that Jaul was the sole
ruler of his immensely rich country in the Arabian Gulf.
She finally understood the arrogance and the authority
that had often set her teeth on edge. Jaul had never been
in any doubt of who he was and where he was going to
end up. No doubt his marriage to Chrissie had just been
a brief fun stop on his upwardly mobile royal life curve
and had never ever been intended to last.

'Proceed with great caution,' Cesare had warned
Chrissie once he had established the exact identity of
the man whom she had married in such secrecy two
years earlier.

That recollection had made Chrissie's skin turn clammy beneath the sleek turquoise shift dress she had borrowed from her sister's pre-pregnancy wardrobe. Her shrewd brother-in-law had pointed out that Jaul would have diplomatic immunity, that he was firm friends with several influential members of the British government and that he would have much greater power than most foreign non-resident husbands and fathers might have if it came to a custody battle. *Custody battle*—the very phrase struck terror into Chrissie's bones. Cesare assumed that Tarif—all adorable fourteen plump and energetic months of him—would now be heir to the throne of Marwan, which would make him a hugely important child on his father's terms. As Chrissie's fear grew in direct proportion to her anxious thoughts, her spine stiffened and her skin grew even chillier. On some craven, very basic level she didn't want to even try to be civilised; she simply wanted to snatch her kids from Lizzie's luxurious nursery and flee somewhere where Jaul couldn't ever find them again.

Instead, however, Chrissie reminded herself that she was supposed to be an adult and able to handle life's more difficult challenges. She mounted the front steps of the monstrous building with its imposing columns, portico and innumerable windows and pressed the doorbell.

Jaul was lunching in a dining room decorated in high 'desert' style circa nineteen thirty by his English grandmother and marvelling at her sheer lack of good taste. He didn't want to pretend he was in the desert and sit cross-legged like a sheep herder in front of a fake fire; he wanted a table and a chair. Mercifully his personal chef and other staff had travelled with him and the service and the food were exemplary. It didn't quite make up though for having to sleep in a bedroom decorated like a tent on a ginormous bed made of rough bamboo poles literally lashed together with ropes. Of course, he conceded wryly, the distractions of the extraordinary décor of the royal home in London served to keep his thoughts away from how Chrissie had looked in shorts with those impossibly long and perfect legs on full display.

Ghaffar, Jaul's PA, appeared in the doorway and bowed. 'A visitor has arrived to see you without an appointment—'

Jaul suppressed a groan and waved a dismissive hand. He was in London on a private visit and had no desire to make it anything else. 'Please make my apologies. I will see no one.'

'The woman's name is Whitaker—'

Jaul sprang upright with amazing alacrity. 'She is the single exception to the rule,' he incised.

Chrissie tapped her heels on the marble floor of the giant echoing hall full of what looked like a display of actual mummy cases from an Egyptian tomb. It was creepy and the lack of light made it even creepier. Staring at a two-headed god statue did nothing for her nervous tension, only ratcheting it up a degree or two and making the events of the past twenty-four hours all the more challenging to bear, never mind accept.

Without warning, Jaul appeared in a doorway and he seemed almost as strange to her bemused eyes, his tall, lean physique sheathed in an exquisitely cut light grey business suit. The only other time she had seen him in a suit had been on their wedding day and she stared, reckoning that that formality didn't detract an ounce from his dark, exotic appeal.

'Chrissie,' he said with a level of gravity that unnerved her, for it was a quality that she had only glimpsed in him at the worst moments of their relationship when he had proved how very serious he could be when she crossed him. 'I was not expecting you to come here.'

'Well, that makes two of us!' she admitted with an uneasy laugh that sounded raw in the echoing silence. 'But I had to see you in private and this was the most straightforward way of doing it.'

'You are welcome,' he breathed and he snapped his fingers and a servant came out of nowhere and thrust open another door while bowing and scraping. 'We will have tea and be...*polite*?'

Colour ran up to the roots of her pale, shining hair. To her horror, her throat developed a lump, emotion swishing through her again in an unwelcome and treacherous wave. Lustrous dark golden eyes rested on her and her heart started to go thumpety-thumpety-thump as if she had suffered a really bad fright. 'Yes...polite,' she agreed shakily, longing for the hostile, aggressive edge that had powered her earlier that morning when he had visited. Anger and antagonism had provided a blessed bumper between her and the maelstrom of emotions his appearance had awakened inside her.

'I would've phoned in advance of my arrival had I known your number,' Jaul breathed as if he knew exactly what she was thinking.

Mercifully he couldn't know, she thought wretchedly, searching his startlingly handsome features with an appreciation that felt terrifyingly familiar. So, he's a painting, a perfect painting, she acknowledged with self-loathing, but she didn't have to keep on noticing, did she?

'Perhaps we should exchange phone numbers now,' she suggested and he dug out his phone and took a note of hers while passing her a sleek business card. 'This feels so weird, Jaul...*all* of it.'

'Of course it does. Naturally we have both changed a great deal,' he fielded with a level of smooth assurance that made her want to slap him.

It was a welcome interruption when a knock sounded on the door and someone entered with a tray, followed by another person, who surged forward with a deep bow in Jaul's direction to yank out a small table and spread it with a cloth. A china stand loaded with miniature French fancies and tiny scones was put on display and the English tea was poured.

The sight shot Chrissie back in time to what she supposed had effectively been her first date with Jaul although she had not seen it as such at the time. He had taken her to an exclusive hotel for afternoon tea, a quintessentially English tradition he had naively assumed everyone followed. Feeling like a lady of the manor, she had very much enjoyed the experience.

'You *remembered*,' she told him without thinking about what she was saying.

But Jaul *hadn't* remembered. Afternoon tea had been his grandmother's routine and it was still served all these years on because the house had never benefitted from another mistress. The faintest colour scored his high cheekbones as he was shot back in time to recall that long-ago afternoon after he had finally persuaded Chrissie to see him as a normal educated male rather than a womanising party animal. She had been wearing a blue dress then as well. The dress had had tiny little flowers all over it and she had sat there, tense and shy with her beautiful hair falling to her waist, and he had been so *scared* of saying or doing the wrong thing and frightening her off again. Scared of what a woman might think for the one and only time in his life! He wanted to laugh at that recollection of his younger, less cynical self but now he was looking at Chrissie again, noting the silvery hair that was shoulder length now, the fined-down line of her perfect features, and other reactions were overwhelming him.

Images that Jaul had resisted for two years were suddenly leaping out of the box he had locked them in. Colliding with the bright turquoise eyes that he knew could turn feverish with longing for him, he went rigid recalling that incredibly erotic eagerness, nostrils flaring, dark eyes shimmering gold beneath his lush black lashes.

The atmosphere had become suffocating, Chrissie registered in dismay, shifting off one restive foot to the other. She met his intense gaze and froze, her temperature running cold and then hot until melted honey pooled low in her pelvis, an almost forgotten sensation from the past. But it was too late by then for her to draw back because Jaul was unexpectedly in front of her, close enough to touch and literally just grabbing her with two strong arms to weld her into sudden highly provocative contact with his lean, powerfully hard body. Air exploded into her lungs as she snatched in a startled breath.

'Chrissie…' Jaul husked, lean hands sliding down

her slender spine to tilt her hips into an even more intimate meeting.

And as she recognised and felt his erection below their clothes, the long, thick evidence of his need hard against her belly, an ache of near pain stirred between her own legs. Her head swam, clear thought forgotten, knees suddenly as weak as bendy twigs. He took her mouth with all the passion she had never forgotten, fiery and urgent and wildly demanding. She took fire from the kiss, which was like a flame hitting bone-dry hay, and the piercing arrow of bittersweet hunger travelled to the very core of her being. Her hands flew up to his broad shoulders and roved from the hard muscle there to the thick blue-black hair she had loved to bury her fingers in.

His tongue plunged between her parted lips and a shudder racked her in his arms, sudden wickedly strong need loosed inside her to run amok like bush fire. She wanted to rip his shirt off and run her hands down over his washboard abs. She wanted to drag him down to the rug below their feet and satisfy the hollow ache screaming at her feminine heart. It was powerful, it was seductive and she could no more have resisted that savagely strong hunger than she could have resisted his explosive passion. She wanted, she *wanted*…

CHAPTER FOUR

SOMEONE KNOCKED ON the door and Jaul froze, literally *froze* as if someone had hit an alarm bell. He pushed her back from him, dark eyes glittering tiger gold and a ferocious frown on his lean, darkly handsome face.

'I'm sorry,' he said flatly. 'That was a mistake.'

Chrissie was unable to pull herself together quite so quickly and as he released her she pivoted away from him towards the windows. As she raised trembling hands to press to her suddenly clammy cheeks, she was sick with self-loathing and shock and only dimly aware that someone was speaking to Jaul in his own language at the door. Feeling shaky, she sat down on a horrendous carved wooden sofa without even a cushion to soften its hard, unyielding seat.

A *mistake*? How demeaning to be told that! Only a kiss, only a stupid kiss, she was reasoning with herself in a daze of shame and denial. But how could she have let that happen, particularly when she had visited him to discuss the infinitely more important reality of the twins' very existence? It was as though something had momentarily stolen her wits, overpowering all memory and rationality in the same moment. Well, what was done was done and *he* had been equally guilty of inappropriate behaviour, she reminded herself in consolation. Of course, she had once been accustomed to Jaul's distinctly carnal can't-keep-my-hands-off-you nature, had indeed at one stage gloried in her apparent power to attract him, innocently assuming that it meant more than it did. It seemed in that line though he hadn't changed a bit.

Jaul was receiving a lengthy message from his PA. He was taken aback to be invited to a legal meeting the following morning between the legal firm chosen by Bandar and the lawyers who would apparently be arriving to represent Chrissie's interests. After her attitude to the divorce issue the night before he was disconcerted but less surprised by her unexpected visit. Had she already thought better of her behaviour? Evidently she could muster a crack divorce team virtually overnight. Perhaps she had also mulled over the financial advantages of giving him the divorce he wanted, he reasoned sardonically. When had money come to mean so much to her?

It was a question he had asked himself repeatedly two years earlier when she had accepted his father's pay-off to turn her back on their relationship and walk away. How had he missed out on that devious, greedy streak in her make-up? At the time he would have described her as the least mercenary woman he had ever met. Had she cunningly concealed her avaricious side from him in an effort to impress him? When they had been together she had gone to great lengths to prove that his wealth meant little to her. And if he was honest, he *had* been impressed because by that stage he had become bored with women who valued him for what he was worth rather than for the man he was.

Yet the woman he had valued beyond all others had proved to be the greediest of all. That was a lowering truth he hated to recall for it exposed his poor judgement when he was at the mercy of his libido. A reminder he evidently needed, he conceded darkly, acknowledging without much surprise that one look at Chrissie's beautiful face and slender but shapely proportions could still arouse him.

Chrissie was finally wondering how on earth she could broach the subject of Jaul being a father and increasingly it was sinking in for her that it would come as an enormous shock to him. Her fingers dug into the clutch bag Lizzie had pressed on her and in a sudden movement she bent her pale head and snapped it open to withdraw the birth certificates. Those documents were self-explanatory and there was really no need at all for her to start stumbling into an awkward announcement.

Chrissie extended the certificates. 'I'm sure you're wondering why I came here.' *Not to kiss you and dream about ripping off your clothes again,* she completed inwardly while her face burned with mortification. 'I had to see you because I thought you should see *these* first...'

Another frown drawing together his fine ebony brows, Jaul grasped the documents with an unhidden air of incomprehension. She hadn't mentioned the kiss and he was grateful for that, well aware of Chrissie's ability to throw a three-act drama over what he viewed as trivia. Time had shot them both back briefly into the past and that was all. Nothing more need be said, he was thinking while he grasped the fact that for some peculiar reason his estranged wife had given him a pair of birth certificates.

'What are these?' Jaul scanned the name of the mother and went cold. 'You have children?'

'And so do you,' Chrissie advised thinly. 'You got me pregnant, Jaul.'

Jaul stilled and stopped breathing. *Pregnant?* The word screamed at him. It was not possible in his mind to credit it at that first moment, but now his quick and clever brain was checking dates, making calculations, recognising that whether he liked it or not it was a possibility. A possibility he didn't want to think about though. He had children, a boy and a girl. The concept was so shattering that he literally could not think for several tense seconds. The woman he was planning to divorce was the *mother* of his children. Inwardly he reeled from that revelation, instantly grasping how that devastating truth would change everything. *Everything!*

But why was he only learning about something as incredibly important as the news that he was a father over a year *after* the event of their birth? Jaul was not accustomed to receiving the kind of shock that rocked his world on its axis. Momentarily he closed his eyes before opening them to stare at Chrissie...beautiful, deceptive Chrissie, who had hit him with an own goal of mammoth proportions.

'If this is true...and I assume that it is,' Jaul framed with the greatest difficulty he had ever had in controlling both his temper and his tone, 'why am I only being told about the existence of my son and daughter *now*?'

Of all the reactions he might have had and she had envisaged while the taxi ferried her across London, that particular one had not featured. It was a Eureka moment for Chrissie and she didn't need to leap out of a bath to be galvanised into instantaneous rage and jump to her feet. 'Is that all you've got to say to me?' she shouted at him full force.

Innumerable generations of royal ice stiffened Jaul's spine, for no male had been more minutely trained from childhood than he had been to deal with a sudden crisis without any show of unseemly emotion or ill-judged vocal exclamations. 'What were you expecting me to say?' he enquired.

The door burst open and all four of his bodyguards rushed in to stare at Chrissie in disbelief. As collected as ever, indeed as if such interruptions were part of his normal life, Jaul sent them into retreat with the instruction that on no account was he to be disturbed again. He knew what had happened: his highly anxious protection squad had heard her shout when *nobody* shouted at him and had feared that some sort of a dangerous incident was developing. But they were nervous and on edge, having never been abroad before and London was a very scary place as far as they were concerned.

Turquoise eyes glittering with rage, Chrissie knotted her fingers into fists. 'Well, maybe I expected something a little more human and you asked me a very, *very* stupid question!'

Jaul gritted his strong white teeth. 'Stupid how?'

'You asked me why you're only finding out about Tarif and Soraya now and I want to ask you…is that a joke?'

'No. It was not a joke,' Jaul responded with perfect diction, studying her with assessing dark eyes. 'Why would I joke about it? Try to calm down and think about what you're saying. This is a very serious matter.'

And that was the moment when Chrissie lost even the slight hold she still retained on her temper. The father of her children was poised there like a granite pillar and acting as coolly and politely as though they were discussing the weather. It was too much, too great an insult after that offensive question to be borne in silence. *How dared he ask her to calm down?* How dared he talk down to her when he had just about wrecked her life and abandoned her to sink or swim?

'You complete bastard,' she breathed in a raw undertone, barely able to get the harsh syllables past her parted lips. '*Why* weren't you told? You *deserted* me—'

'I did not—'

'You went back to Marwan and you never returned to me—that's desertion. You didn't answer your phone. You didn't call, email, write, even text…I never heard another word from you!' Chrissie slashed back at him shakily, bitter wounding memories surfacing inside her head to power her on. 'You left me no way of contacting you. Of course I appreciate now that that was deliberate because you *knew* before you left that you weren't coming back—'

'That is untrue—'

'Shut up!' Chrissie practically screamed at him, her sense of injustice and furious hurt too great to be silenced now that she finally had Jaul in front of her. 'Don't lie to me! At least be honest…what could you possibly have to lose now?'

His lean, devastatingly handsome features clenched hard. 'I have never lied to you—'

'Well, the "love you for ever" bit was certainly a lie! Telling me that the Oxford apartment was *our home* when your father could throw me out of it at a moment's notice was a lie! And according to him even our *marriage* was a lie!' she reminded him, half an octave higher, and it did not help her mood when Jaul visibly winced. In punishment, she snatched up a sugar bowl and flung it at him, sugar cubes flying like tiny missiles as the china bowl shattered on the edge of a small table.

Jaul was right in the middle of the three-act drama he had hoped to avoid. Urging calm wasn't working, listening quietly wasn't working either. But then all that had ever worked with Chrissie when she was angry was dragging her off to bed until they were both thoroughly satisfied. That was a totally inappropriate thought, he admitted, struggling to concentrate on what mattered most: the children. But how could children he had never heard of until this day or even seen seem real to him?

'Thanks to your father's little "mistake", Jaul, my children are listed as illegitimate and without a father!' Chrissie ranted, almost running out of breath but quickly powering up for the next. 'Now my family may not be from a culturally conservative place as sensitive as Marwan but my father didn't speak to me for over six months once he realised that I was pregnant and unmarried because he was ashamed and embarrassed—'

If possible Jaul froze to an even greater extent.

Having been convinced by King Lut that she was *not* a married woman, Chrissie had not had the power to put Jaul's name on the birth certificates as to do so he would have had to accompany her to the register of births to register their birth or have made a statutory declaration that he was the twins' father. Chrissie had also been afraid to mention a marriage that she had already been told was illegal, fearful that in some way she might have accidentally broken the law by going through with such a ceremony. She had also been very much afraid of the risk of attracting embarrassing publicity should the royal status of her children's father ever become public knowledge. Anonymity and silence all round had seemed the safest option after her fruitless visits to the Marwani Embassy.

'In fact if it hadn't been for my sister and her husband, I would've been in even more serious trouble than I already was. So don't you *dare* ask me why you weren't told that you were a father when you were such a very lousy husband or non-husband or whatever you were!' Chrissie slung tempestuously.

'Is that it?' he enquired, dark eyes glittering bright as a starry night. 'Are you finished hurling abuse?'

'That was not abuse…that was what happened!' Chrissie raved back at him, undaunted. 'Do you know what your problem is?'

Jaul knew he was about to find out.

'People don't stand up to you, don't expect you to account for the wrong you do because you're this super rich, powerful guy who's spoilt. I hate you. I absolutely *hate* you!' Chrissie shouted at him, punctuating the assurance with the milk jug that had accompanied the sugar bowl. 'You're a horrible, seducing, selfish, womanising rat!'

'I think you should go home and lie down for a while. I'll phone you later when you've calmed down a little,' Jaul murmured without any expression at all and it just made her want to scream until she was carried off and locked away as the madwoman the Marwani Embassy staff had once treated her as.

Chrissie was rigid with fury: Jaul had no idea what hell she had gone through, probably even less interest, and she very much doubted that he had absorbed what she had told him.

Pregnant, Jaul was still thinking in a daze, trying and failing to imagine Chrissie's slender figure swollen with his children, Chrissie going through the pregnancy alone while rejected in disgrace by *her* father as a single parent. For the very first time he was glad she had had the money his father had given her, even relieved by the idea because she would have needed financial support. Children, he thought again, unable to imagine them, a baby boy and a baby girl, the first twins in the royal family since his grandfather and great-uncle's birth. Dimly, he realised that he was in such deep shock that he was in an abnormal state of disorientation and detachment, completely divorced from his usual cool, rational mind.

'Just you try lying down for a while when you have two babies of only fourteen months old to look after!' Chrissie hurled as a last-ditch put-down, stalking out of the door. She ignored the fact that his bunch of bodyguards were pacing the hall like worried parents having heard the noise of shouting and breaking crockery. They rushed past her to check that their precious charge, the King, was unharmed. King indeed, she thought incredulously, for that Jaul had become a king had just never seemed real to Chrissie.

A servant rushed to open the front door to her, visibly eager to see her off the premises. If they mentioned her name at the Marwani Embassy they would all be able to get together and talk about what a raving nut job she was, the crazy Englishwoman who wept and shouted and begged. Well, that wasn't her any more because she had soon got over loving Jaul. When a man ditched you as cruelly as Jaul had ditched her, there was no coming back from such an experience. Nothing had ever hurt so much… She flung a disgusted glance back at all the shining windows of that weird mansion and if she had had a brick in her hand she would have thrown that as well.

Jaul was frozen in the doorway, only marginally conscious of his large staff now grouped in the hall to study him in consternation, desperate to know what had caused such a fracas in his deeply traditional household.

And what Jaul did next would very much have stunned Chrissie.

'Miss Whitaker is my wife…my Queen,' he announced with quiet dignity in his own language, ignoring entirely the utter shock spreading across every face turned towards him.

Chrissie went back to her sister's home and cried again, tears dripping down her face as Tarif looked up at her with his father's eyes and smiled.

Lizzie hovered, understandably unsure of what to say. 'It can't have gone that badly,' she insisted. 'Did he insist there would have to be DNA tests and stuff like that to prove the twins are his?'

'No, nothing like that. I shouted at him and threw things at him while he stood there like a stone statue,' Chrissie recounted bitterly. 'There was no satisfaction to be had out of it at all. I wanted to kill him.'

Lizzie had paled. 'I'm sure relations between you will settle down eventually. Right now, Jaul's probably in shock—'

'What's he got to be in shock about?' her sibling asked thinly.

'Discovering that he's a father—'

'I hate him. I'm going to go out tonight and have

fun with Sofia and Maurizia,' Chrissie swore, springing upright and dashing the tears from her eyes. 'Jaul stole all that away from me!'

Lizzie knew that was true but she deemed it wiser to say nothing. Chrissie had had a very hard time while she was carrying the twins because it had not been an easy pregnancy and all the pastimes of youth had been lost to her. Her little sister had had to grow up too soon and face heartbreak and betrayal at a time when all women were very vulnerable but that she had done so without a single whine of self-pity and had gone on to establish a career in teaching had made Lizzie feel incredibly proud.

It would have been a challenge to know which of the parties was the most surprised when Jaul showed up at Lizzie and Cesare's home that evening.

Lizzie hovered and hurriedly called her husband, feeling that Cesare would be politer and more diplomatic than she could be when forced to deal with the detestable man who had married her sister and let her down so badly.

'I would like to see Chrissie…' Jaul announced without a shade of discomfiture.

'Unfortunately that's not possible,' Cesare declared smooth as butter. 'She's out—'

'*Out?*' Jaul repeated in apparent surprise.

'Clubbing,' Lizzie supplied with pleasure.

'Then I would like to see the twins,' Jaul advanced grimly and Lizzie enjoyed a first-hand experience of the stone-statue image Chrissie had employed.

Cesare sighed. 'I'm afraid that's not possible either. I

couldn't let you see the children without their mother's permission—'

Jaul's gaze flamed bright gold. 'They are *my* children—'

'But it doesn't say so on their birth certificates, does it?' Lizzie cut in with unashamed satisfaction. 'You'll have to come back tomorrow when Chrissie is here—'

'Where has she gone...*clubbing*?' Jaul asked with distaste.

And to Lizzie's annoyance, Cesare gave Jaul information that she would have withheld.

'Why on earth did you tell him?' she demanded when Jaul had driven off again in his glossy limousine adorned with official Marwani flags.

Cesare shot her a sudden unreadable look that disconcerted her. 'He's Chrissie's husband.'

'But she *hates* him!'

'It's not our place to interfere. Making an enemy of him isn't likely to help anyone and least of all their children, *cara mia*,' he reasoned.

Escorted into the plush VIP area of the exclusive club, Jaul was restless. His bodyguards had perked up though, he noted with a sudden amusement that pierced his exasperated mood. His protection team was overjoyed to be in what his father would have described as a 'Western den of iniquity'. He stood on the balcony overlooking the dance floor packed with scantily clad girls below but his thoughts were far removed from the sight.

Chrissie's family disliked and distrusted him and in the wake of the chaos his father had created that was hardly surprising, Jaul conceded grudgingly. Even so, such a poor reception struck at his pride and his sense of honour for in twenty-eight years of life he had never once shirked his responsibilities. With the exception of Chrissie, he acknowledged bitterly, running through all the reasons why that had happened. He cursed his own pride and vanity for not finding some way to make enquiries of his own and check out what his father had told him.

Yet such misgivings about his only parent would never have occurred to Jaul before. Jaul had been very close to his father and positively coddled. A man who had virtually panicked whenever his only child succumbed to common childhood illnesses was not a man to inspire distrust. Jaul tucked the memories away hastily, working through the bitter bite of his lingering grief for the older man while feeling disloyal about the vague doubts that Chrissie's condemnations had stirred up.

Instead Jaul found himself wondering how often Chrissie came to such clubs. He told himself that in the circumstances that was none of his business. Unhappily, traits stronger than reason and a bred-in-the-bone possessiveness for what was *his* quarrelled with that rational conviction. He was hoping that she had more clothes on than women normally wore in such places. He was also already questioning the wisdom of having followed her to such a venue. He had acted on an angry impulse, an urge that rarely led to a satisfactory conclusion. And in the same second that he was about to leave the club he saw her, a bright figure in a short fuchsia-pink dress accompanied by two other young women. She was laughing, smiling, clearly not in turmoil, he noted, gritting his teeth at the sight. He wondered why he was agonising when she, so patently, was not.

Blessing her foresight in their exchange of numbers,

he texted her, watched from above as she literally froze, full pouty pink mouth down-curving, shoulders tensing. Annoyance licked through Jaul's long, lean frame at the clear message that his presence was as welcome in the club to her as a marauding gorilla's. He summoned the waiter to order champagne and snacks.

Rage crackled through Chrissie when she read the text.

Please join me in the VIP section

Her one night out on the town in months and Jaul had to ruin it by reminding her that she was not as free as the other young women around her. Suddenly she wished she had a man in tow, rather than being with Cesare's sisters, who were simply excited to death to be invited to the VIP section. But no, whether she liked it or not she was Jaul's wife and the mother of his children and telling him to get lost wouldn't work because Jaul was relentless about getting his own way.

Once she had believed that Jaul was incredibly solid and trustworthy and honourable. She had virtually worshipped the ground he walked on and remembering that now made her feel nauseous. But then, to be fair, the night their relationship had at last changed into something more at university, Jaul had played a blinder, she recalled numbly.

She had finally started dating someone while still suppressing her attraction to Jaul with all her might. Adrian had been blond, blue-eyed and sporty and as different from Jaul as day was from night. She had gone out with Adrian several times, enjoying casual dates in cinemas and cafés and telling him no when he got too pushy about sex. Back then she'd had a complex about sex and hadn't known or much cared whether she would ever get over it because it had stemmed from something sordid that had frightened her when she was still a child. And she had never told anyone, not even Lizzie, about that sleazy secret.

Adrian and his mates had taken her to a party in a big house and at some stage of the evening her memory had shut down. She suspected Adrian had put something in her soft drink and it had been Jaul who had found her slumped by Adrian's side and clearly out of it. He had stepped in to rescue her because he had known that, like him, she didn't touch alcohol. Jaul had punched Adrian when he'd tried to object and had carried her out of the party. She had no recollection of the rest of the night, only of waking up the next morning to find herself safe in Jaul's apartment. For the first time she had seen another side to Jaul. He hadn't taken advantage of her. He had stepped in to look after her when she'd needed help, had protected her from what could have been a very nasty scenario, making her suddenly painfully aware that he was miles more mature and decent than many of the young men she met. All her prejudices against him had crumbled that same day.

'I would never hurt you,' he had murmured.

But that had proved the biggest lie of all. She was so angry with him, *still* so angry with him, she acknowledged ruefully, but what was the point of all that aggression so long after the event? Their marriage was dead and gone—that was the end result. Let it all go, put it away, she urged herself wryly, let him have his divorce and move on to a better, happier future. Their lawyers would be meeting tomorrow: the divorce would soon be rushed through for Jaul's benefit.

Chrissie sank into the designated comfortable seat right in front of Jaul and wondered why his bodyguards were bowing in her direction as if she were a real somebody. She looked amongst them for two familiar faces, but the men who had once protected Jaul in his university days were not there. Turning back to Jaul, she noticed that he was casually dressed, had actually got in wearing jeans and an open-necked white shirt, proving the point that entry to such exclusive clubs depended more on *who* you were than what you wore. The white of his shirt against his golden skin tone was eye-catching and a deeply unsettling tingle quivered through her slender body when she connected with his brilliant dark golden eyes surrounded by lashes longer and more luxuriant than her own. He *was* gorgeous, no point denying that, she allowed, her keen gaze tracking the lean, strong lines of his masculine features while she tried not to wonder who he was planning to marry *next*...

Chrissie wasn't stupid. After all, that was obviously why Jaul was in London in the first place talking about needing a divorce and fast. While he was planning to marry wife number two, he had discovered he was *still* married to wife number one. How very inconvenient, she thought bitchily while Sofia and Maurizia stared goggle-eyed at Jaul and sat down at a table across the way to happily tuck into the champagne and snacks laid out for them.

'I hope my arrival has not disrupted your evening,' Jaul remarked stiffly, striving not to react to his ringside-seat view of her long, perfect legs crossed, little feet he had kissed shod in glittery pink high heels.

With difficulty he dragged his attention up to linger on the lovely face he knew so well, willing back the almost instantaneous surge of blood to his groin with an actual prayer for self-control.

'Of course not,' Chrissie lied, angling her pale head back, shimmering hair swishing across her shoulders like silk as she strove to be gracious for the sake of peace. 'I assume you wanted to see me about something?'

Jaul confided that he had gone to her brother-in-law's home in the hope of seeing the twins.

Chrissie was disconcerted. 'You want to see Tarif and Soraya?'

Jaul elevated a fine ebony brow. 'And that surprises you?'

Chrissie reddened in sudden severe mortification. She had told him he was a father and *obviously* he was curious. To have assumed that he would simply accept that news and walk away again had been sheer folly, she conceded ruefully. 'I could bring them on a visit tomorrow morning,' she suggested, prepared to show willing in the civilised stakes. 'Before the lawyers kick in—'

'The lawyers?' Jaul repeated as if he didn't know what she was talking about.

'The divorce meeting,' Chrissie leant forward and whispered, endeavouring to be tactful in the presence of the bodyguards who, it seemed, had not taken their eyes off either her or Jaul since the moment she'd sat down.

Jaul recognised the restrictions of the meeting place he had chosen and cursed his inability to speak freely. He expelled his breath on a slow hiss. At least she was speaking to him again, at least she wasn't shouting, he reasoned grimly.

'Cesare's legal team will soon get it all sorted out,'

Chrissie told him on an upbeat note intended to offer comfort. 'He says they've dealt with much more complex stuff than this.'

Jaul's veiled dark gaze glittered and dropped down to the bareness of her left hand. 'What did you do with the rings I gave you?' he asked softly.

'They're in Cesare's safe. I was keeping them for Soraya,' Chrissie responded, wanting to let him know that she had not retained them for any sentimental reason.

'They have Arabic names—'

'A nod to their heritage,' Chrissie cut in carelessly.

'My grandfather was called Tarif—'

'It's pure coincidence,' Chrissie declared deflatingly, lying through her teeth because she *had* named her son after his grandfather, reasoning that her baby had the right to use a name from the royal family tree. 'I never would have dreamt of naming them after anyone in your family.'

In receipt of that snub, Jaul wanted to punch the wall and shout, but he mastered the surge of anger with a silent, strong self-discipline honed by long months in a hospital bed and even longer months of painfully slow rehabilitation. She hated him; his wife *hated* him. He could sense the animosity still bubbling away below her newly calm surface, could see the sharp evasiveness in her beautiful eyes.

He had brought this hellish situation down on himself, he decided harshly. Two years ago he had still been immature and impatient and reckless. He had taken what he'd wanted without hesitation and without thought of the risk he could be running...

CHAPTER FIVE

'THEY LOOK CUTE as buttons,' Lizzie said fondly, studying the twins garbed in their smartest outfits. 'Jaul will fall in love with them at first sight.'

Chrissie wrinkled her nose. 'I hope not because he's not likely to see much of them when we live in different countries. I also hope he's not always going to be asking me to put them on planes to go and see him.'

Her sister breathed in deep. 'Chrissie…I know it will be difficult but you should *want* him to be interested in his son and daughter, no matter how awkward it is for you. A father in their lives would be a plus, not a minus.'

Duly admonished for her honesty, Chrissie flushed and climbed into the limousine that Jaul had insisted on sending to collect them. She was thoroughly disconcerted to see that he had actually sent his bodyguards as well. She knew Lizzie had spoken sensible words but the prospect of sharing the twins with Jaul daunted her. He was the man she had once loved beyond bearing and the idea of her children being looked after by his next wife in Marwan chilled her. But that was the way the world was now with families and step-families and ideally everyone being relaxed about once bitter relationships that were in the past, she reminded herself irritably. Other people coped and she would have to learn to cope as well. Even so, she couldn't help thinking that it would have been easier altogether if Jaul had never come to London and had never had to be told that he was a father.

The front doors stood wide open on the massive house for their arrival. As she clutched first Tarif below one arm and then struggled to hoist Soraya, a woman in a nanny uniform came running out and offered to help.

'I'm Jane,' she announced. 'Your husband sent me out to assist.'

Chrissie was unimpressed that Jaul was too proud and exalted to come and help her with his own hands but she allowed the woman to lift Soraya. They walked into the hall and on into the ugly drawing room where the nanny deposited Soraya on a new fluffy rug covered with brand-new toys and asked if there was anything Chrissie needed for the twins.

'No, thanks. I have everything I need with me.' Chrissie settled her sizeable baby bag down on one of the wooden sofas and wondered where the heck Jaul was.

But when she looked up from settling Tarif down on the rug Jaul was in the doorway, garbed in black designer jeans and a dark red T-shirt and looking very much like some elite male supermodel from his stunning cheekbones all the way down to his sleek, beautifully built body. The thought shook her and her cheeks went pink, heat trickling through private places, reminding her of intimacies that were no longer part of her life.

'I'm sorry. I was taking a call.' Jaul moved to the edge of the rug and just halted there to stare at the twins with blatant curiosity. 'I don't know anything about babies, which is why I brought the nanny in to prepare for their visit.'

'You must've met some babies?'

'No. There are none in the family…well, there *is* no family, only me,' he reminded her, for he had no siblings and neither had his father and so there were no other family branches to join with his.

'Tarif and Soraya are your family now,' Chrissie heard herself point out and then wondered why she had said that, but there was something strangely touching about his confession of complete ignorance. 'Just get down on your knees and they'll come to you.'

'They can walk?' Jaul was entranced when Tarif made a beeline for him and crawled up onto his lap with a fearless expectation of being welcomed there.

'No, they're only crawling.' Soraya saw her brother receiving attention and headed in the same direction. 'They're starting to occasionally pull themselves upright…Tarif more than Soraya.'

Jaul smoothed Tarif's black hair back from his brow. His hand wasn't quite steady. *His* children! He still could not credit the evidence of his eyes. 'For that night they were conceived…I thank you,' he breathed huskily.

Chrissie glanced across at him and her face flamed as though he had lit a fire inside her. They had run out of condoms and Jaul had wanted to send one of his staff out to buy more and she had been furiously embarrassed by the idea, angry that he would not go on such an errand for himself. So, they had taken the risk and the twins were the result. His expression of gratitude now, however, shook her by its very unexpectedness.

Slowly, Jaul began to relax. The twins responded to his demonstrations of various toys with smiles and laughter and gurgles and they put everything in their mouths. 'They're wonderful,' he told her quietly.

'Yes…I think so too,' Chrissie said with a grin. 'Most parents think their kids are wonderful.'

It felt like a time out of time for Chrissie, for the presence of the children muted her hostility to Jaul and her tension had ebbed. 'They need a nap now,' she announced, scrambling upright intending to leave, a slender figure in jeans and a purple tee.

Jaul hit a button on the wall. 'There are cots upstairs ready for them. Jane will come.'

Chrissie stiffened. 'But I was about to go back home…'

'We have to talk. We might as well do so while our children sleep,' Jaul retorted smoothly as if it was no big deal.

Chrissie didn't want to talk to him though. She thought it was much better to let the lawyers handle everything and keep the dissolution of their sadly short little marriage unemotional and impersonal. On the other hand, she didn't want to be unreasonable and wondered if he was really hoping to see more of the twins after their nap. She climbed the stairs behind Jane, each of them cradling a twin.

An entire nursery had been assembled for the babies' use and she wasn't surprised—even a few short weeks living with Jaul had taught her that with sufficient money almost anything could be achieved overnight. Once Tarif and Soraya were settled she walked slowly downstairs again.

Jaul was in the drawing room and a fresh tray of coffee awaited them. Chrissie shot a rueful glance at it. 'You're a brave man,' she commented, thinking of the sugar bowl and jug she had hurled on her previous visit.

'You couldn't hit a wall at six paces,' he teased, a

slow grin curling his strong, sensual mouth and chasing the gravity away entirely, giving her an unsettling glimpse of the slightly younger, lighter-hearted Jaul she had married.

'Aren't we being civilised?' Chrissie remarked in turn while she poured the coffee and offered him a cake like the perfect hostess.

'Perhaps you should put the cup down now,' Jaul advised, poised straight and tall by the window. 'Because I don't want a divorce.'

Her turquoise eyes flew wide and her coffee cup rattled against the saucer she held. 'I beg your pardon?'

Jaul breathed in very slow and deep, broad chest expanding below the T-shirt. 'If the children are to take their proper place in the royal family I cannot give you a divorce now,' he explained tautly. 'I *can* get away with producing a wife and children like rabbits out of a hat and people will understand because my father's prejudice against Western women was well-known. But for the sake of the family and my country I cannot throw in an immediate divorce—'

Without the smallest warning, Chrissie felt ready to scream with vexation because it seemed to her that they were programmed to be at odds with each other. She had lain awake the night before remembering how she had foolishly threatened to make getting a divorce difficult for Jaul and she had seen no sense in taking such a stance. Surely it was wiser for her to agree to a quick divorce and move on with her life? Why the heck would she want to prolong that process and leave herself neither married nor single purely for the sake of causing Jaul some temporary aggravation? In the end she had decided that a quick divorce would be best for both of them, particularly if she was going to have to share the twins with Jaul.

'I'm sorry,' Chrissie now said flatly. 'But I *do* want a divorce and I can have one whether you like it or not. I'm afraid I don't owe you or your country anything—'

Jaul shifted a graceful hand in a silencing motion. 'Perhaps I phrased this in the wrong way. I'm asking you to give our marriage another try—'

Chrissie set down her cup with a jolt and stood up. 'No,' she said, refusing to even think about that suggestion. 'Too much of my life has been screwed up by you and I want my independence back—'

'Even if it's at the cost of your children?'

'That's not a fair question. I have done everything possible to be a good mother—'

'Tarif is the heir to my throne. I *must* take him home with me,' Jaul murmured very quietly. 'I do not want to part him from you or his sister but it is my duty to raise my heir—'

Chrissie's knees wobbled and every ounce of colour had leached from her drawn cheeks. He was talking about taking Tarif back to Marwan as if that were already a done deal. Did that mean he had already established that he had that right? Her stomach dive-bombed and her throat convulsed. 'I can't believe I'm hearing this. You're asking me to give our marriage another go because you want the kids, not me—'

'Don't be stupid,' Jaul urged with sardonic bite. 'I wanted you back the moment I laid eyes on you again. You're like my "fatal attraction" in life and I very much suspect that that works both ways.'

'And what's that supposed to mean?' Chrissie demanded tempestuously, breasts heaving below her top.

Lustrous dark eyes flickered pure gold. 'You want me too,' Jaul framed silkily. 'You want me so much you're eaten up with it and I'm the same—'

'That's the biggest piece of nonsense I've ever heard!' Chrissie proclaimed furiously.

'You need me to prove it?' Jaul launched back at her, dark eyes blazing threat.

'You couldn't prove it because it isn't true!' Chrissie argued. 'I've moved on way past you…'

'In what way?' Jaul demanded.

Her temper was jumping up and down inside her like a screaming child because she had suffered so much because of him and that he should show up again and start laying down the law about *his* wants, *his* needs was too much for her to bear.

'I've been with other men,' she lied with deliberation, knowing how possessive he was, how jealous, how all-consuming his passion could be…and knowing just how to hurt.

'I expected that,' Jaul framed in a harsh undertone. 'You didn't need to spell it out—'

But Chrissie had watched him pale below his vibrant skin and it made her feel like a total bitch, especially when she was lying, but it seemed so important to her right then to drive a wedge between them, to prove that she was completely free of him and what they had once shared. 'So, you see, I don't want you the way I once did.'

Burning bright golden eyes trailed over her from the crown of her head right down to her curling toes and she felt her body react the way it always did around Jaul. Her breasts swelled in a bra that suddenly felt too tight, her nipples pinching taut while lower down she felt hot and moist.

'And you are one hundred per cent certain of that, are you?' Jaul seethed as he stalked closer. '*So* certain you won't even give me a chance?'

Chrissie snatched in a ragged breath. The atmosphere was smouldering like a combustible substance and the tension was suffocating because she recognised that Jaul was on the edge of his hot temper, which when lost was considerably more dangerous than her own. 'Yes, I'm certain,' she told him stubbornly.

'You're a liar,' Jaul told her harshly. 'You're lying to me—you're even lying to yourself! We've been down this route before—'

'I don't know what you're talking about—'

'Oh, yes, you do, *habibti*,' Jaul contradicted. 'I'm talking about the months you made me wait for you—'

'I didn't *ask* you to wait—'

'You turned your back on the attraction between us. You refused to acknowledge it.'

'Well, I didn't think you were *my* kind of person and…oh, yes, didn't I turn out to be right about that?' Chrissie boxed back without hesitation.

'Stop it,' Jaul grated, locking both arms round her to haul her up against him.

'No, you get your hands off me…*right now*!' Chrissie snapped back angrily. 'We're getting a divorce and you're not allowed to touch me!'

'You're still my wife.'

'But you don't get to touch!' she warned a split second before his beautiful mouth, warm and wet and rawly sexual, came crashing down on hers in an electrifying collision. His tongue pressed in deep.

For a split second she imagined she saw a shower of sparks because the taste of Jaul's mouth on hers was as wildly exhilarating as hitching a ride on a rocket ship. Her legs went numb and her body hummed like an engine cranking up after a long time switched off, pulses like static tightening her nipples and warming her pelvis. It happened that fast, that her reaction was so strong it almost blew her away. Her hands slid up his arms, holding him to her, every skin cell in her body alight in a blaze.

She had told herself that it wouldn't be like that if she touched him again. She had told herself that the response she recalled was the result of infatuation, exaggerated by an imagination reluctant to let go of the sparkly romance that had turned into car-crash viewing. But she had lied, not knowingly, but out of ignorance and wishful hopes because the discovery that Jaul could still deliver a kiss that could set her on fire was downright terrifying.

Struggling to catch her breath, she looked up at him, into eyes dark and glittery as a starry night, and for a split second of madness she wanted to drown there and turn time back in its tracks. Instead, she rested her cheek against a broad shoulder, breathing in the musky, clean scent of him like a hopeless addict. He smelled so good, he smelled so *right* that it frightened her. She quivered, insanely aware of every line of his long, lean body against hers and the terrible wanting rising inside her like a drug haze she couldn't possibly fight and win against. 'Jaul?'

Long brown fingers cupped her cheekbones. 'Give me your mouth again,' he husked.

No, that wasn't going to solve anything and she knew it, but still she tilted her head back like a programmed doll and he kissed her again, longer and deeper, harder

and stronger and her senses went spinning off into a
fantasy land of rediscovery. It had been so long, far too
long since she had even had a kiss and what could be
said about a kiss? she scorned inwardly. A kiss was no
big deal even with an estranged husband and he was
so good at kissing, so wickedly erotic he should have
been bottled and sold like precious oil. He lifted her up
against him with that easy strength of his that had once
thrilled her to the marrow. He hitched her legs round
his waist, nuzzled his mouth against her throat where
she was, oh, so sensitive, oh, so responsive, and suddenly her whole body was vibrating like a tuning fork,
greedily reaching for every sensation and drinking it in.

Her eyes were tightly closed as if what she didn't see
didn't have to be accounted for. This wasn't her doing
this and letting Jaul carry her upstairs. This wasn't what
she wanted but, oh, dear heaven, how much she wanted
him! That mad, frenzied wanting was throbbing and
pounding through her as unstoppable as a runaway
train. She buried her face in his shoulder in despair at
her own weakness.

'I can't do this…I *can't*,' she whispered feverishly.

In an awkward movement, Jaul nudged her head up
and found her mouth again, briefly, devastatingly. 'Yes,
you can, because in your heart you know I will never
hurt you again.'

'It's not that simple—'

'It is as simple as you will allow it to be,' he growled,
his breath fanning her cheek.

But nothing was ever that simple with Jaul, her brain
reminded her. Sometimes he was too clever, too devious for her, while she was a straight-down-the-line open
and honest person. He pushed a door open and then he

kissed her again and carnal heat engulfed her in an irresistible tide, washing away every thought.

She was lying on something soft and yielding and
above her Jaul was virtually ripping off his T-shirt,
smooth brown pectoral muscles rippling down washboard abs before her eyes. And seeing that beautiful
body again was too much temptation all at once because
her hands rose of their own volition and smoothed up
over that torso from the vee rising out of the loosened
waistband of his jeans to the narrow waist and up over
the lethal strength etched into the sleek lines of his
hard, muscular chest. The heat of him burned her palms
and a clutch of longing pulled in her belly. Desire was
like an old familiar stranger, controlling her, silencing
her, heightening the craving to a dangerous level. She
couldn't have him, she *shouldn't* have him, but the hunger was intolerable and more than she could withstand.

He came down to her again, hot and half naked, peeling off her top and then her bra, filling his hands with
the pouting mounds of her breasts, fingers grazing her
tightly beaded nipples and tugging them before he put
his mouth there with hungry urgency. Her back arched,
arrows of flaming need slivering through her quivering
length to the heart of her. Sweet sensation tugged at her
with every suck of his lips, every lash of his tongue,
and then he kissed her again and her fingers knotted
in his black hair. Tiny little sounds broke in her convulsing throat as he tugged off her panties and traced
the swollen flesh between her thighs. A single finger
pierced her and she cried out, already so hot, so ready
she was wet and oversensitive.

'Don't wait,' she heard herself mumble, wanting,
needing, strung on a high of anticipation.

But Jaul never had been a male prone to following instructions in bed and he teased her first, toying with the tiny button of her desire so that she gasped and her hips jerked and her legs flailed and what remained of her control was ruthlessly wrenched from her. He shimmied down the bed and used his mouth and his tongue on her most tender flesh. From that point, she no longer knew what she was doing, was positively enslaved by the wanton hunger beating like an angry drum inside her, pushing her responses higher and higher until her whole body convulsed on a bitingly fierce climax, wave after wave of almost forgotten intense pleasure pounding through her weakened length.

'That's one,' Jaul husked with his unforgettable confidence, dark eyes shimmering gold pools of hunger as what remained of his clothing went sailing across the room. He tore the corner from a small foil pack with his teeth and came down to her, lean brown powerful body arching over hers with balletic grace and all the hard, driving promise of extravagant pleasure she had learned to expect from him.

I'm not doing this, I'm not really *doing this,* she reasoned crazily with herself, still intoxicated by the physical gratification she had denied herself for too long. The long, slow, torturous glide of him into her damp sheath was irresistible, stretching sensitive tissue before sinking deep in a deliriously energising thrust. She strained up to him and she couldn't help it because excitement was powering her and he was moving, hard and fast, sending ripples of deliciously dark erotic sensation travelling through her lower limbs. His rhythm was the blinding white heat of passion and she was lost and defenceless against the erotic moves of his lithe, strong body, caught up in the moment and reaching desperately for the highest peak with every sobbing, gasping breath. And then the scorching, blinding heat splintered into ecstasy as potent as an explosive charge and she cried out as the voluptuous, spellbinding pleasure expanded and flooded her with sweet sensation in the aftermath.

Afterwards, Chrissie wasn't even quite sure where she was because Jaul was still holding her close and that felt both familiar and strange and she didn't know how to react to it. Instead she lay there like a stick of rock, barely breathing, under attack from a roaring grip of discomfiture. On the very edge of the divorce that she had told him she wanted she had slept with him again. Humiliation engulfed her and powered her into pulling free and rolling over in silence to the other side of the bed.

Powered by no similar onslaught of self-consciousness and regret, Jaul got the message and sprang out of bed. 'We start again,' he pronounced with decision as he stretched, his long brown back rippling with muscle in the sunlight.

And somehow the very fact that it was still daylight and that her innocent children were napping somewhere in the huge house made Chrissie feel even more guilty and conflicted than ever. In that turmoil of uneasy emotion she almost didn't notice the scarring on Jaul's back as he strode towards what she assumed to be the bathroom. Striated silvery lines marked his spine and she frowned, momentarily sidestepping her other anxieties to say abruptly, 'How did you get the scars on your back?'

'In an accident...car,' Jaul told her flatly.

As he stood there, naked and brown and gorgeous, his perfect profile turned towards her, she wondered if he had always had the scars and she simply hadn't noticed them. How observant had she been of his back view? she asked herself wryly, dismissing her momentary concern to let the other feelings of confusion and self-loathing engulf her again.

'I still want the divorce,' Chrissie told him stonily.

His strong jawline clenched. 'We'll discuss it after I have a shower.'

'OK.' Like someone desperate to pull clean linen over a mistake, Chrissie was eager for him to get dressed and leave her free to do the same.

'There's another shower off the room next door,' Jaul remarked tautly. 'I'll use it.'

'Your bodyguards aren't standing outside the door, are they?' Chrissie checked.

'They'll be downstairs.' Jaul sent her a perceptive appraisal from grave dark eyes. 'It is not their business to monitor or discuss my private life and they know it well.'

Chrissie was scarlet to her hairline, could feel her very cheeks throbbing with unwelcome heat. 'I'll use the other shower,' she said quietly.

'We are married. There is nothing to be embarrassed about,' Jaul murmured soothingly.

He strode into the bathroom releasing Chrissie from paralysis and she fled from the bed, snatching up clothes, pulling them on any old way before creeping from the room and literally tiptoeing into the bathroom next door to make use of the facilities. But washing didn't noticeably make her feel any better. She had insisted that she wanted a divorce and then fallen into bed with him again and now he thought he had her exactly where he wanted her. Was that so surprising?

Chrissie would not have put it past Jaul to have deliberately set out to get her horizontal. He was no slowcoach with women, no fool when it came to what mattered. His passion was irresistible but he would know perfectly well that she would feel tormented by what had just happened between them and he probably felt quite self-satisfied because he had proved *his* point: she *did* still want him and crave him in the most basic of ways.

That meant more to Jaul than it meant to her though. When she had first met Jaul he had been a sexual predator, programmed to take advantage of willing women even though he had not behaved that way with her. In fact, although they had hit astonishing highs in the lesser intimacy stakes, Jaul had *married* her before he actually had full sex with her, making her appreciate even back then that in some ways Jaul was much more anchored in his own culture than she had ever properly appreciated. It had also made her wonder in low moments after he had disappeared if she had won Jaul purely by saying no for so long and thereby acquiring all the glorious lustre of a challenge and a worthwhile trophy. Was that the simple explanation of why the heir to a Gulf throne had chosen to deem an ordinary Yorkshire girl special enough to marry? But then had he ever planned on it being a permanent marriage?

But that past was long gone and she was over it, Chrissie reminded herself as she got dressed again. Just not as over him as she had thought she was, a little inner voice reminded her deflatingly. Jaul would think he had won now, would assume she would become his wife again. It probably was just that basic for him, his belief that if she had sex with him again it meant he had her back.

And whose fault was it that he would now be thinking that? Chrissie boiled with regret inside herself. Pure naked lust had overwhelmed her. It was a fallacy to believe that only men could react like that, she ruminated unhappily, a nonsense to assume that a woman couldn't feel the same way. She had never been with anyone other than Jaul but she had learned a lot about that side of her nature even in the short time they had actually lived together and knew that she was a passionate woman. And the only reason she hadn't slept with anyone else since Jaul was that she had yet to meet any male who had the same highly charged sexual effect on her that he did.

Jaul towelled himself dry after a shower with a reflective look on his lean, strong face while he tried to work out whether he had made the right or wrong move with Chrissie. She was so stubborn, so unforgiving. Did she have genuine cause to feel that way?

He refused to believe that his late father had lied to him, so what point was there in making enquiries at the embassy? Such an investigation into King Lut's behaviour would be downright disloyal and it would be sure to spawn unpleasant rumours and damaging gossip. His features sombre at that prospect, Jaul cursed below his breath. He had a wife. He had two children. He might have spent two years in ignorance of those facts but the reality was that now he had to live with his wife and his children in the present and not in the past, harking back to old disruptive issues that only roused bitterness and aggression in both of them.

She had taken the money and run. Did he continue to hate her for that even when he now knew that she had been pregnant and in dire need of financial help? She was younger than he was, less mature and all of a sudden he hadn't been there for her. A woman of greater selfishness might have had a termination rather than raise two children she had not planned to conceive. Whether he liked it or not, fate had ensured that he had let her down by not being there for her when he had been needed.

And on a much lighter note, he ruminated abstractedly, shapely mouth sultry with recollection, the sex was amazing. But where once it had been the icing on the cake, now it was the only glue likely to give them a future as a couple. Wasn't that why he had swept her off to bed? That laced with unashamed desire, of course.

Why was he even thinking like this? In the past, Chrissie had often made him think about stuff that generally struck him as not quite masculine and when they were first married he had resented that truth. He was not a knight on a white charger like some character out of the medieval romances she had once adored. He had never pretended to be perfect but he had always known that she wanted him to be that knight. Chrissie the realist was deeply intertwined with Chrissie the romantic.

And now he was about to be the bad guy again, he acknowledged grimly. He had no choice. He had not had a choice from the moment he'd learned of his son's existence.

Chrissie was brushing her hair when she heard the guest-room door open and she stiffened, leaving down

the brush and walking to the bathroom door. Jaul was
in jeans and a bright turquoise tee that clung to his im-
pressive chest and if she felt lacerated by what had occurred, he looked infuriatingly energised, she reflected
wretchedly.

'I thought we should talk in here,' Jaul confided.

Less risk of being overheard by his staff, she trans-
lated. So, what was he about to tell her that she might
want to shout and scream about?

'I still want the divorce,' she repeated doggedly.
'What happened just happened but it doesn't change
my mind about anything.'

Burnished golden eyes shaded by luxuriant black
lashes surveyed her without perceptible surprise. 'We
have a link we could still build on—'

'I don't think so,' she argued, waving a pale, slender
hand in a dismissive gesture. 'Been there, done that. I
could never trust you again and let's face it…you wanted
a divorce as well until you found out about Tarif. I appreciate that Tarif's birth changes things for you but it
doesn't change them for me.'

'And that's your final word on this subject?' Jaul
pressed with sudden severity.

Chrissie lifted her chin, refusing to let mortification take over. She had made a mistake but that didn't
mean she had to live with it and build her entire future
around it. 'Yes, I'm sorry, but it is…'

'Then perhaps you should look at *this*…' Jaul slid a
folded document out of his back pocket and held it out
to her. 'I didn't want to be forced to make use of it. I had
hoped to avoid it because coercing you is something I
would've preferred not to do. But this particular document would have been produced by my lawyers had

any divorce meeting taken place,' he explained flatly. 'However, I have cancelled that meeting.'

'What on earth is it?' Chrissie whispered anxiously.

'It's the pre-nuptial contract you signed before we got married,' Jaul informed her levelly. 'I don't think you read it properly.'

The vaguest of memories stirring, Chrissie wrenched open the sheet of paper and saw the clause marked with a helpful red asterisk in the margin. Her heart in her mouth, she read the clause relating to the custody of any children born of their marriage in which she had agreed that any child they had would live in Marwan with Jaul.

Her mouth ran dry because she vaguely remembered reading that more than two years previously and cheerfully dismissing the concept from her mind because it had not seemed remotely relevant to her at the time. After all, they had not been planning to start a family immediately and the prospect of babies and the problems of custody should their marriage run aground had seemed as remote as the Andes to her back then. They had been madly in love, at least *she* had been in love and, trusting and naive soul that she was, it had not occurred to her that some day in the not too distant future her blithe acceptance of that clause might come back to haunt her…

CHAPTER SIX

HE HAD TRIED to play nice, Jaul reflected grimly, but nice hadn't panned out too well with Chrissie, who was suspicious of his every move and had ensured that they were now down to the brutal bare bones of legal agreements and custody. Possibly he wasn't very good at playing nice, he acknowledged in exasperation, having much more experience of playing nasty. The King's word was the last word to be heard in serious disputes in Marwan and there was always an aggrieved party, convinced of unjust treatment and favouritism. He had learned that, regardless of negotiation and compromise, someone would always be dissatisfied with his decision.

Like a drowning woman forced to review the most important moments of her life, Chrissie was pale as death as she stared down at that clause in the pre-nuptial contract. Her heart was sinking down to the very soles of her feet. She could not see how she could possibly combat an agreement that she had voluntarily signed.

Jaul breathed in slow and deep, muscles rippling below the T-shirt, wide shoulders taut. 'At some future date, should you remain *convinced* that you want a divorce—'

Her turquoise eyes flared back to life like the unholy blue hot streak flickering inside a flame. 'You'd better believe that I won't change my mind!' she traded furiously.

'Then you will be entitled to your own household in Marwan in which to raise the twins. I'm afraid that is the best I can offer you should you want your freedom back,' Jaul imparted grittily, white teeth flashing bright against golden skin.

'But…for the moment, a separate household for the three of us is out of the question?' Chrissie prompted dangerously.

'I'm afraid so. At least this way, however, you retain shared custody of our children,' Jaul pointed out.

'They've never been *our* children, they've always been *mine*!' Chrissie vented painfully, biting back a flood of recrimination.

'Only because I didn't know I was a father,' Jaul parried.

'And what you refer to as "this way" means that you expect me to pretend that we still have a real marriage?' she interpreted jaggedly as she stalked to the door and spun back again. 'How could you do this to me after deserting me for two whole years? Don't you have any moral decency?'

'It is not that simple for me. In an effort to secure our children's status and acceptance by my people, I'm prepared to pretend I'm part of a happy couple. That's part of my duty of loyalty and care towards them and their needs,' Jaul framed in a raw undertone. 'They will take their place in the royal family as the prince and princess they are and that *is* my responsibility *and* yours.'

Yanking open the guest-room door, Chrissie was reckoning that she could have done without the parental slap on the wrist. He scarcely needed to remind her of the maternal obligations that had consumed her youthful freedom throughout the time they had lived apart. It was so unfair, she thought bitterly, that Jaul could have walked out on her, abandoning *his* responsibilities and then walk back into her life only when it suited him to demand that she observe a duty of care that he had royally ignored.

'Will you agree to it?' Jaul asked, striding after her impetuous exit to follow her down the corridors that led to the giant upper landing.

Adrenaline on a high, her steps faltered while common sense and survival instincts took over. The twins had become a weapon and if she wanted to keep her children she had no other option but to take up residence in Marwan.

On one level she recognised the position he was in, on another she hated him for making it her responsibility as well. It was one thing to own up to a two-year-old marriage and two young children and shock the Marwani population but it would be another thing entirely to stage that shock along with a headline-grabbing divorce in the UK while they fought a bitter custody battle over their children. Because, no matter how damning that agreement she had signed would prove to be when aired in a courtroom, Chrissie knew she would still fight for her children regardless. But such a fight would undoubtedly damage everyone involved.

Did she really want to land the stress of a custody battle on Cesare and Lizzie as well? Hadn't she already caused them as much grief as a wayward teenager with her exam agonies, touchy pride, carefully kept secrets and unplanned pregnancy? Did they really deserve to have to deal with more on her behalf? Shouldn't she be handling her own problems and standing on her own feet? Wasn't that really what adulthood was all about?

'Chrissie…?' Jaul prompted, falling still. 'I need an answer.'

'I'll do it because I don't appear to have the choice of doing what I want,' Chrissie shot back at him tightly. 'But I won't forgive you for it.'

Brilliant dark eyes veiled, his beautiful mouth compressing. 'You've never forgiven me for anything I did wrong.'

Chrissie refused to believe that was true. She must have forgiven him at some stage for something. She was not a hard, unforgiving person, was she? Her first impressions of Jaul returned to haunt her and, along with it, her long-held refusal to consider the fact that she might have misjudged him. Very faint colour warmed her cheeks.

She recalled that she had never forgiven her mother for what the older woman had put her through and frowned. Francesca had died before her younger daughter reached the age of confrontation and the older woman had taken her guilty secrets to the grave with her. Chrissie swallowed hard, struggling to shake off the dirty, shamed feeling that always engulfed her when she thought of Francesca. She was older now, wiser and less judgemental, she reasoned tautly. Her mother had not been a strong person and she had been very much abused in some of her relationships with men. Her second husband, the very last man in her life, had been the worst of all, taking advantage of Francesca's weakness and dependency on him to propel her into an unsavoury lifestyle. Some day she might tell Lizzie the truth about their mother, but certainly she could never ever imagine sharing that sordid story with Jaul.

'I think this is an incredibly weird and ugly house,' Chrissie remarked curtly on the way down the massive staircase, which reminded her of something out of an ancient Hammer Horror movie. It only lacked zombies sidling out of the mummy cases in the hall to totally freak her out.

'Blame my grandmother. She furnished this place.'

'The Englishwoman who walked out on your grandfather?' That was the bare bones of what Chrissie knew about her British predecessor in the Marwani royal family. 'Tell me about her.'

'Why?'

'Fellow feeling…aren't I sort of following in her footsteps?' Chrissie quipped, eager to talk about something, *anything* other than the agreement she had just given and what had occurred in the tumbled sheets upstairs. That extraordinary passion had left her aching in intimate places and even walking wasn't quite comfortable. Jaul had been so…wild and forceful…and she had revelled in that display of primal passion, but now she was being forced to pay the piper and put her whole life back in Jaul's hands. She should never have let herself down like that, she thought painfully. He was running rings round her now.

'I hope not. She deserted her son,' Jaul proffered censoriously. 'She met my grandfather Tarif on a safari in Africa. She was a socialite from an eccentric but aristocratic English family…Lady Sophie Gregory. Tarif fell deeply in love with her but he was simply a walk on the wild side for her…a novelty. A couple of months of life in backward Marwan where there were no ex-pats for company was too much for my grandmother. She stayed only long enough to give birth to my father and walked out only weeks afterwards.'

Chrissie knew when she was listening to a biased story. 'This is what *your* father told you?'

'Yes. I met her once though when I was a teenager. I was in Paris on an officer training course and she was at a party I was invited to,' Jaul told her grudgingly. 'She came right up to me and said, "I understand you're my grandson. Are you as stiff-necked and stubborn as your father?"'

'So, your grandmother *did* try to see her child again,' Chrissie worked out wryly from that greeting. 'In other words she wasn't quite as indifferent a mother as she was painted to you. Most probably your grandfather wouldn't *allow* your grandmother to see her son again because she walked out on their marriage. Have you ever thought of that angle?'

Jaul *hadn't* and his jawline clenched like granite because that particular family story had long been an incontestable legend set in stone and he couldn't credit that Chrissie had already come up with a likelihood that had never once occurred to him. 'There were grounds for his bitterness.'

'Such as?' Chrissie was receiving a twist of satisfaction from needling Jaul even if it was only about old family history. Why? He was wrecking her life again. He *owned* her, just as he owned their son and daughter. There was no leeway for misunderstanding in that clause in the contract, no wriggle room for a screamingly naive girl who had been so in love she hadn't foreseen a future where she might have children and end up alone and abandoned. She knew she would never forgive herself for being that stupid and that short-sighted about so very important an issue as the right to keep and raise her own babies and live where she chose.

'Lady Sophie's desertion made Tarif a laughing stock. In those days saving face was everything for a ruler but there was nothing he could do to hide the fact that *she* had left him.'

'And no doubt he never forgave her for that and kept her from her son as punishment while brainwashing that same child into a hatred and distrust of Western women,' Chrissie filled in with spirit, her disgust palpable. 'Don't forget I met your father and I was left in no doubt that he saw a woman like me as a curse on his family name. Knowing how he felt, why on earth *did* you marry me? No, scratch that, don't answer me. I *know* why you married me.'

Fine ebony brows pleating, Jaul was recalling their final argument in Oxford. She had wanted him to take her out to Marwan with him, had protested the secrecy he had insisted on and had implied that his attitude bore a closer resemblance to shame than secrecy. But that was untrue. He had known that without preparation and forewarning his father would react badly and he had flown home intending to break the news of his marriage in person. Sadly, he now knew that he should have made the announcement much sooner and had he done so he was convinced that everything that followed would have happened very differently.

'You don't know why I married you because you never have known what I was thinking,' Jaul boxed back cool as ice water. 'In reality, I was trying to protect you but, unhappily for both of us, I went about it the wrong way.'

A lift door whirred back in the hall and the nanny, accompanied by a young woman in Marwani dress, appeared, each bearing a beaming drowsy twin back to their mother.

'I'll leave now.'

'I want you to stay,' Jaul decreed.

'Listen.' Chrissie rested a hand daringly on a muscular brown forearm as she stretched up to him to whisper, 'For now, I'm staying with my family. I'll do what I have to do only when you leave for Marwan. When is that happening?'

'I have to return within twenty-four hours. I have already released the photos taken at our wedding at the embassy to the press at home.'

Chrissie lost colour. Only one wretched day of freedom left? Only *one* day more to be with her family and savour her independence and liberty to do as she liked. 'So you expect me to…what?'

'Close down your life here in the short term. Your family will naturally be welcome to visit and stay with us whenever they like.'

'Then it's about time you met my father,' Chrissie pronounced abruptly, a rueful expression in her eyes for she doubted that Jaul would enjoy the experience. Her dad was chock-full of prejudices, against foreigners, rich people and royalty to name only a few, and Brian Whitaker was not diplomatic about hiding the fact. Jaul deserved that meeting as she had not deserved hers with his late father, Lut. 'He's coming down to London tonight to visit us.'

On the way back to her sister's with the twins, Chrissie was recalling the day she had met King Lut, remembering the clammy break of sweat on her skin when she had finally grasped the alarming truth that the angry older man, dressed exactly as though he had stepped off a desert film set, was actually her father-in-law. He had not even spoken to her in English. Throughout another older man had stood anchored to his side translating his every furious gesture and bitten-out word and yet Jaul had once told her that his parent spoke fluent English. Possibly the King's temper had prevented him from finding the right words in her language, the horrible, hateful words that had never left her once he had assured her that their very marriage had been completely unlawful...

'It was *not* a proper marriage. It was never intended to be more than a casual affair and Jaul wants to be left in peace. It is *over* between you now that he's back in Marwan. He does not want you living here in his English home, nor does he want to hear from you again. Please do not embarrass him further by visiting our embassy. My son plans to marry a decent woman from his own culture and who will marry him if you cause a scandal?'

There had been a lot more along the same lines, Chrissie recalled unhappily, every word aimed at ensuring that she accepted just how unimportant she was and how unfit she was to be Jaul's wife. She had been a sexual fling, nothing more, an intruder in his apartment, an embarrassing visitor creating scenes at the embassy, in short a woman pitifully clinging to a man who no longer wanted her. Her pride had been crushed and her heart broken because she had loved Jaul with all her heart.

And now it seemed that her life had turned full circle, she reflected as the limo whisked her back to her sister's home. She knew that Cesare and Lizzie would support her if she chose to fight Jaul for the children but she could not help recalling that even Cesare had urged her to be cautious in her dealings with Jaul, because Jaul had more power and influence than the average non-resident father. In other words even her powerful and extremely shrewd brother-in-law had been doubtful of her chances of winning such a custody battle.

And there were *two* menacing sides to her dilemma, she acknowledged wretchedly. If she fought Jaul it would turn bitter and nasty and then what would happen if she ultimately lost the custody battle? How much would Jaul allow her to see of her children in the hostile aftermath of such a conflict? She shivered, clammy and cold inside as she pondered that very realistic question. Hadn't she already had the warning of learning what had happened to Jaul's British grandmother, Lady Sophie? From what she could establish that poor woman had never got to see her child again, at least not until he was an adult and too locked into his prejudices and hostility to listen to the other side of the story. Chrissie reckoned that if she wasn't careful she might fall victim to the same heartbreak and lose her children altogether.

Her other concern was the sheer selfishness of plunging Cesare and Lizzie into that same conflict with her. Lizzie was pregnant again and the very last thing she needed was added pressure and anxiety. A court case would be nerve-racking and would attract the sort of publicity that her sister and brother-in-law abhorred, for in spite of their wealth they led quiet, private lives. However, if Chrissie plunged into a divorce and custody battle with Jaul, the press were sure to pick up on it because an Arab king's secret marriage to an English-woman would be all too newsworthy to ignore. No, she couldn't possibly risk exposing her family or her children to that kind of intrusive publicity. They all deserved better from her, she conceded heavily. After all, she had chosen to marry Jaul and the consequences were hers to deal with. Why should anyone else pay the price?

CHAPTER SEVEN

CHRISSIE SAT ON Jaul's private jet during the flight to Marwan like a small grave statue, slender body straight-backed and rigid, hands circumspectly folded on her lap, eyes veiled.

Jaul compressed his sensual lips and grimly returned his attention to his laptop. What had he expected? A relaxed and happy travelling companion? It was wiser to concentrate on the positives: Chrissie was on board with his children and, even better, was considerately wearing the sort of outfit for her first public appearance that would impress his people. The simple blue shift dress enhanced the slender grace of her figure. In the sunlight coming through the porthole behind her, she looked incredibly beautiful with her hair gleaming like a liquid fall of bright reflective silver. That same exacting light accentuated her almost transparent porcelain skin and the lush perfection of her soft pink lips.

All too fast and predictably, Jaul recalled the silky brush of her hair across his thigh and the hot, erotic grip of her mouth. Long brown fingers braced on the table edge in front of him as arousal coursed through him with the force of a volcanic flow of lava, leaving him hot and hard and throbbing with need. Gritting his teeth, he concentrated instead on thinking about how she would react to the special request he had to make of her. He compressed his wide, sensual mouth, resolving to approach the topic with tact.

Chrissie's stillness cloaked her inner turmoil. She wanted to scream and shout with angry frustration. Jaul had, quite literally, hunted her down and trapped her like prey. Two years too late she was taking up the role of being his wife and the mother of his children, a role that she would once, most ironically, have eagerly embraced. A trickle of perspiration beaded her short upper lip as she recalled the incredible crush of paparazzi fighting to photograph the Marwani royal party at the airport and the sheer wall of security men it had taken to hold them back. It had not occurred to her that their marriage would so quickly incite that amount of attention. Jaul had taken it in his stride but Chrissie had been unnerved by that level of public exposure.

But then, in truth, the past twenty-four hours had been equally unsettling. Cesare and Lizzie had reacted to her announcement that she was returning to Marwan with Jaul with far less surprise than Chrissie had naively expected. Her sister and brother-in-law had assumed that Jaul and Chrissie were making an effort to rebuild their marriage for the sake of their two young children.

'And if it doesn't work out, at least you know you tried and you can come home again,' Lizzie had proclaimed in her innocence of the fact that 'coming home' was an option that Chrissie had legally surrendered two years earlier. To come home, she would have to be willing to leave her children behind her and that was not an option she could ever imagine choosing.

That same day, Chrissie had boxed up her possessions for storage and had put her apartment in the hands of a rental agency. For what had remained of her meagre twenty-four hours of freedom, she had gone shopping with her sister for a more suitable wardrobe of formal clothing. In the evening her father had arrived in London for a visit and Jaul had joined them for dinner. Jaul had dealt calmly with her father's often barbed comments and he had laughed when Chrissie had remarked on his discretion before his departure.

'When it comes to temperament, your father is a walk in the park. My father lost his head in rage at least once a week. There was no reasoning with him and he would often say offensive things. Of course, he was very much indulged growing up and because he saw himself as an all-powerful ruler he never studied to control his temper,' he had confided, startling her with his candour. 'It was a good learning experience for me.'

That glimpse into Jaul's background had sharply disconcerted Chrissie because to her it had sounded less like a learning experience and rather more like living with a tyrant. Recalling the raging man she had once briefly met, Chrissie had made no comment as she suppressed an inner shiver while contemplating the possibility that, with such an intolerant and inflexible parent, Jaul's childhood could not possibly have been as secure and privileged as she had always assumed.

Before boarding the flight, Chrissie had gone to a beauty salon to have her hair trimmed and her nails painted, small measures to enable her to present herself as the well-groomed royal wife people would be expecting to see by Jaul's side. *Royal?* That very word made her roll her eyes. The only royal thing about her was that she had allowed Jaul to *royally* shaft her in every sense of the word, she thought with rebellious bitterness.

She had agreed to return to a husband who had once abandoned her and who had yet to explain himself on that score. How on earth had she allowed him to get away with that? How had she let that huge question get buried beneath her terror of losing custody of the twins? And what the heck was Jaul *still* hiding from her?

He was probably only trying to hide the unlovely truth from her, Chrissie reasoned with scorn. But she wasn't stupid and she could work out the most likely scenario for herself. Obviously Jaul had *never* loved her; all he had ever felt for her was lust, a lust honed to a fine sharp edge by the length of time he'd had to wait to get her into bed. Had he realised soon after their marriage that he had made a dreadful mistake and that she was not at all what he wanted in a wife?

Had he then confessed all to his father? Why else would Jaul have never returned from Marwan? Was he now ashamed of having once treated her so cruelly? Of the fact that he had dumped her without even having the guts to tell her he was done with her? Of the fact he had had his father pay her off as though she were some sort of slutty gold-digger? Was that why Jaul had still to explain his own behaviour?

From below her lashes, Chrissie studied her husband with simmering intensity. Whether she liked it or not, dressed in a charcoal-grey suit stamped with the flaw-less cut and fit of handmade designer elegance, Jaul looked absolutely gorgeous. One look at him with his strong jawline already shadowed by faint black stubble and his guarded dark eyes pinned to her below the heavy black fringe of his lashes and her pulses hammered. She had a sudden devastating image of his lithe, sleek body sinking down over hers and, even in the mood she was in, her breathing constricted and her heart pounded like crazy. Jolted by that response, her chest tightened in a stress reaction even as she felt her nipples prickle and swell below her clothing.

In Jaul's magnetic presence those reactions came as naturally as breathing to her. Her carefully constructed barrier of scorn was already being burned off by the pool of heat spreading like liquid honey at the heart of her. It was desire, the very same lust she had mentally slated Jaul for, and it was a terrifyingly strong hunger, she acknowledged grudgingly, and unfortunately not a stimulus that died down at her bidding. If she didn't watch out and stay on her guard, he would hook her in again like a stupid fish.

But why on earth did she feel so cringe-makingly needy? She had lived perfectly well without sex until Jaul came back into her life and now it was as though he had lit a fire inside her that she couldn't put out. That burning hunger unsettled her and flung her back in time to the days when just being near Jaul had swept her up to an adrenaline-charged high where desire and emotion combined in an intoxicating rush. And no way was she planning to let herself sink back to that level, she swore inwardly.

By the time the jet was circling and getting ready to land, Chrissie's tension was on a high. She was apprehensive about the new life ahead of her in Marwan. Naturally she was. A different culture, a language she didn't speak and suddenly she was royal, an actual queen? Of course she was nervous about the mistakes she would undoubtedly make.

Furthermore in her head where it mattered she still saw herself as a Yorkshire farmer's daughter, born in poverty and raised by a troubled mother. She had made it to university and trained as a teacher but it had never once crossed her mind that one day she would be the wife of a king. Even when she had married Jaul she had failed to look ahead to that future because it had seemed so far away and unreal. She had not been aware at the time that, although seemingly in the best of health and looking much younger than his years, King Lut had already been in his seventies. The older man had suffered a massive heart attack and had died without the smallest warning.

'I should tell you that within Marwan the news of our marriage has been received very positively,' Jaul informed her soothingly as the jet engines whined into a turn. 'The palace has been flooded with congratulations, bouquets and gifts for our children.'

Chrissie was pleasantly surprised. 'But surely your people think it's very odd that it took until now for you to admit that you are married?'

'My father's prejudices against Western women and his rages were legendary and people have proved to be remarkably understanding of my reticence,' Jaul confided wryly.

Jane, their new nanny, joined them with the stewardess, the twins clad in white broderie anglaise playsuits for their first public airing. Silence fell as everyone buckled up. Chrissie breathed in slow and deep and resolved to make the best of her new future. A future from which she excluded all thought of Jaul. She didn't have to stay married to him for ever, she reminded herself doggedly. Once they were able to separate, she wouldn't even need to live below the same roof with him, she reflected, studying his bold bronzed profile and wondering why that particular thought was signally failing to lift her spirits.

When it was time to disembark, Jaul lifted Tarif out of Jane's arms. 'I want to show him off.'

'But you wouldn't let anyone photograph the twins in London,' Chrissie remarked in surprise.

'That was London. This is Marwan. Our people have the right to see this little boy in the flesh first,' he decreed without hesitation. 'He is my heir and one day he will be King.'

They disembarked and the line of people waiting to greet them outside began to move closer. Jaul's bodyguards fanned round them lest a crush develop. Somewhere a military brass band was playing and Chrissie was disconcerted to see television cameras set up below the bright blue sky. The heat was intense and it was much hotter than Chrissie had innocently expected it to be. The advance party of VIPs engaged Jaul in conversation and a smiling older woman approached Chrissie, bobbed a curtsy and told her in excellent English that Soraya was adorable. Cameras were clicking and flashing all around them and Chrissie found it stressful to keep on talking and smiling as though nothing were happening. Painfully slowly the royal party and the interested crowd surrounding them made their way into the airport building, which was mercifully air-conditioned.

That coolness was welcome to Chrissie while even more photos were being taken of them indoors. Being the centre of so much attention with the twins was a shock to her system but she was enjoyably surprised by the mood of genuine friendliness at their arrival and the number of people who spoke her own language. When Tarif began to get restive in his arms, Jaul recognised that it was time to move on and within minutes they were ensconced in a limousine, travelling down a wide boulevard. Her eyes widened when she registered the crowds of waving well-wishers. Jaul was evidently a popular ruler. Gripped by curiosity, she gazed out at streets lined with the sort of ultra-modern buildings that might have featured in any city, although the occasional glimpses of elaborate minarets and men in robes added a touch of exotica to the urban landscape.

'What's the palace like?' she asked in the rushing silence.

'It's old-fashioned,' Jaul warned her. 'Everything's as old as Queen Victoria aside of the bathrooms, kitchens and IT connections. It's been generations since the palace had a queen to take an interest in it.'

'I'd forgotten that.'

'You can change anything you like. I'm pretty much indifferent to my surroundings…unless it's completely weird and uncomfortable like the mansion in London,' he conceded wryly.

The limo had left the city streets behind and rocky plains of sand bounded the desert highway. Dusk was falling. Away in the distance Chrissie could see the looming heights of giant rolling sand dunes coloured every tawny shade from ochre to orange by the setting sun. Giant gates dissecting very high turreted walls appeared a hundred yards ahead and Chrissie sat forward with a look of bemusement. 'Is that the palace? My goodness, it's the size of a city and it looks like a Crusader castle!'

'The front part of the original fortress *was* built by the Crusaders before we threw them out,' Jaul volunteered with amusement. 'For hundreds of years as fashion changed every generation added new buildings. Even I haven't been in all of them. The family was once much larger and in those days my ancestors lived with a vast retinue of servants and soldiers, who all had to be housed.'

The guards patrolling the walls were waving their guns and roaring a welcome as the limo purred through the automatic gates.

'So, who's in charge of everything here at the palace?' Chrissie asked curiously as their vehicle passed through glorious landscaped gardens before gliding to a stately halt in front of the ancient main building with its huge domed entrance porch.

'Bandar, my principal aide, is the nominal head because he is in charge of domestic finance but my cousin, Zaliha, actively runs the royal household. Her sister is married to Bandar, who lives here on site with most of my personal staff.'

A smiling finely built brunette with sloe-dark eyes appeared in the doorway and performed a respectful dip of acknowledgement. She introduced herself as Zaliha in perfect English, tendered her good wishes and begged to hold Soraya all in the space of one breath. The welcome cool of air-conditioning engulfing her overheated skin, Chrissie walked into an amazing circular hallway with walls studded with mother of pearl. 'Shells…seashells,' she remarked in disconcertion. 'It's beautiful.'

'There's quite a bit that isn't quite so lovely,' the brunette warned her ruefully.

'Don't give my wife the wrong impression,' Jaul urged lightly.

'You speak incredibly good English,' Chrissie told her companion.

'My father was on the embassy staff in London and I went to school there,' Zaliha told her.

'Oh, my word…' Chrissie was staring into the cluttered rooms they were passing, rooms bulging at the seams with antique furniture, some of which appeared to be centuries old. 'It's worse than Victorian,' she told Jaul helplessly. 'It's more like…*medieval*.'

'And ripe for renovation,' Zaliha told her cheerfully.

'We will go straight to our rooms now,' Jaul countered before the brunette could involve Chrissie in such a discussion and he curved lean fingers round Chrissie's elbow.

'Yes, sir.' Zaliha bobbed another curtsy and went straight about her business.

'I was planning to explore a little,' Chrissie protested in a perturbed undertone as Jaul urged her round a corner and up a stone staircase.

'Later, perhaps. Right now I have something important to discuss with you,' he proffered with unexpected gravity. 'This wing of the palace is entirely ours and private,' Jaul announced as they reached the second floor.

As he opened the door into a clearly newly furnished and decorated nursery, their nanny stepped forward and grinned with pleasure at her surroundings. Two young women hurried towards them to offer their assistance with the twins.

'You and Jane will have to beat off helpers with a stick in the palace. It has been too many years since there were royal children below this roof,' Jaul commented, entwining Chrissie's fingers in his to guide her further down the wide corridor. She was relieved to see that contemporary furnishings featured in the large rooms she passed. Time might have stopped dead downstairs in what she deemed to be public rooms, but in Jaul's part of the palace time had mercifully moved on.

He swung open a door into an elegant reception room furnished in fresh shades of smoky blue and cream and stood back for her to precede him. She slid past him, taut with curiosity while the scent of him flared her nostrils, clean warm male laced with an evocative hint of the spicy cologne that was so uniquely him it made her tummy flip like a silly schoolgirl. Her cheeks burnished with colour at the reflection, Chrissie moved away from him as he doffed his jacket and loosened his tie.

'You said we had something to discuss,' she prompted with determined cool.

'My advisers have asked us to consider staging a traditional Marwani wedding to allow our people to celebrate our marriage with us,' Jaul informed her, knocking Chrissie wildly off balance with that suggestion. 'There would be a public holiday declared. The ceremony itself would be private…as is our way…but we would release photos of the occasion—'

'You're asking me to marry you *a-again*?' Chrissie stammered in shock.

'Yes. I suppose that is what I'm asking.' Lustrous dark eyes flaring gold and then veiling below black curling lashes, Jaul levelled his gaze on her.

Her frown deepened. 'You want us to remarry even though we've agreed only to stay together until you feel a divorce would be acceptable to your people?'

His stunning bone structure tightened, brilliant eyes

narrowing. 'I don't want a divorce. I haven't wanted a divorce from the moment I learned that we had two children.'

Shaken by his proposition, Chrissie sank down onto a sofa before steeling herself to say rather woodenly, 'I don't care about what you want. I only care about what you *agreed*. And you *agreed* that I could have a divorce if I wanted one.'

'But our children need both of us. I grew up without a mother—she died the day I was born. Children need mothers *and* fathers. I want this to be a *real* marriage and not a pretence,' he countered without apology.

Chrissie sprang out of her seat, revitalised by that admission. 'So, you *lied* to me in London. You just said what you had to say to persuade me to return to Marwan with you but clearly you never had any intention of giving me a divorce.'

Jaul stood his ground, wide shoulders rigid, lean, powerful body tense as he watched her pace. 'I did not lie. I merely hoped that you would eventually change your mind about wanting a divorce. Hoping is not a lie, nor is it a sin,' he assured her drily.

A bitter little laugh erupted from Chrissie at that exercise in semantics. 'But you're way too good at fooling me, Jaul. You did it two years ago when I first married you and I trusted you then and we both know how that turned out. Doesn't it occur to you that I could never want to stay with a husband I can't trust? And that going through a second wedding ceremony would only make a mockery of my feelings of betrayal?' she demanded emotively, struggling to rein back her agitated emotions. 'After all, you *still* haven't explained why you left me two years ago and never got in touch again…'

Jaul was frowning and he lifted an expressive hand to silence her. '*Chrissie*, listen to—'

'No.' Her luminous turquoise eyes were bright with challenge and she lifted her chin, daring Jaul to deny her the explanation she deserved. 'No more evasions between us, no more unanswered questions,' she spelt out tautly. 'You have nothing left to lose and you can finally be honest. Two years ago in spite of all your claims of love and for ever, you broke up with me, you dumped me… It is what it is.'

'But that isn't what happened…' In a gesture of growing frustration as the tension rose, Jaul raked long brown fingers through his luxuriant black hair. 'And what is the point of discussing this so long after the event? I want a fresh start in the present—'

'What happened back then is still *very* important to me,' Chrissie stressed, determined not to back down. 'I think you realised that our marriage was a mistake and you couldn't face telling me that to my face—'

'No, that wasn't what happened,' Jaul broke in with sudden biting harshness. 'When I left you in Oxford I had *every* intention of coming back to you. My father had asked for my help and I couldn't refuse it. A civil war had broken out in Dheya, the country on our eastern boundary, and thousands of refugees were pouring over the border. The camps were in chaos and I was needed to co-ordinate the humanitarian effort—'

'For goodness' sake, you didn't even tell me that much two years ago!' Chrissie complained, her resentment unconcealed. 'Did you think that I was too much of an airhead to understand that that was your duty?'

'No, I didn't want you asking me how long I'd be away because when I flew out I really had no idea,'

Jaul admitted with wry honesty. 'I travelled down to the border in a convoy filled with medical personnel and soldiers. A missile fired by one of the factions fighting in Dheya went astray and crossed the border into Marwan. Our convoy suffered a direct hit...'

Chrissie was so utterly shaken by that explanation that she collapsed back down onto the sofa , her legs weak and her heart suddenly thumping very hard inside her chest. 'Are you telling me that you got...hurt?'

'I was the lucky one.' Jaul grimaced. 'I survived while everyone with me was killed. I was thrown clear of the wreckage but I suffered serious head and spinal injuries and I was in a coma for months.'

In the early days of his vanishing act, Chrissie had feared that Jaul had met with an accident, only to discount that as virtual wishful thinking when time had worn on and there had still been no word from him. Nausea now shimmied sickly through her stomach and she felt almost light-headed at the shock of what he had just told her.

'But nobody told me anything. Nobody even contacted me. Why did nobody tell me what had happened to you?' she asked weakly, struggling to comprehend such an inexcusable omission.

'Very few people knew. My father put a news blackout on my condition. He was afraid that my injuries would provoke a popular backlash against Dheya and the refugees. In reality what happened to me was a horrible accident and not an uncommon event on the edge of a war zone,' he pointed out with a sardonic twist of his lips. 'I was still in a coma when my father came to see you in Oxford—'

'You were hurt, you *needed* me...and yet your father

didn't tell me!' Chrissie registered with rising incredulity and anger. 'Obviously he didn't want me to know what had happened to you but I was your wife! I had every right to be with you.'

'Don't forget that my father didn't accept that we were legally married. I had only informed him of our marriage the night before my trip to the camps and he was very angry with both of us.'

'But you were still in a coma when he came to see me,' she reminded him, her eyes darkening with disgust when she considered that aspect. 'Your father actually took advantage of the fact that you were unconscious. How low can a man sink?'

Lean dark, startlingly handsome features grim, his dark eyes sparking gold at that challenge, Jaul breathed curtly, 'He was trying to protect me, but I do not and never will *condone* his interference.'

'Oh, that's good to know!' Chrissie countered with biting sarcasm. 'He kept your wife away from you when you needed her—very protective, I don't think!'

Jaul was tempted to remind her that his father had offered her money to walk away from their relationship and forget she had ever known him and that after that meeting with his father she had agreed to do exactly that. But now that he knew that she had been pregnant and had given birth to his children, he saw the past in a very different light. She would very much have needed that money to survive as a single parent and he could no longer condemn the choice she had made.

'So, you were in a coma,' Chrissie recounted stiffly, mastering her raging rancour over his father's behaviour with the greatest of difficulty because she knew that insulting the older man would only cloud and confuse more important issues. 'When did you come out of it?'

'Only after three months when they had almost given up hope. I didn't remember you at first. I didn't remember much of anything,' Jaul admitted heavily. 'I'd had a serious head injury and I was in a very confused state of mind with only fragments of memory all jumbled up inside my head. My memories returned slowly. My father told me that he had seen you and given you the money. He also reiterated his belief that our marriage was invalid and informed me that you would not be coming to visit me.'

Chrissie had turned pale as white paper because rage was storming through her in an almost uncontrollable surge. Had she known that Jaul was in hospital, *nothing* would have kept her from his side! But while he had lain in that hospital bed, his father had manipulated the situation and played on her ignorance of the accident to destroy a marriage he had abhorred. How could even the most loving son deem that a 'protective' act? King Lut's interference had been wicked, indefensible and cruelly selfish. The effort of restraining the hot temper and hostility mounting inside her made Chrissie feel sick.

'I hate your father for what he did to us!' she snapped back at Jaul in a small, tight explosion of raw emotion that could not be suppressed. 'He intentionally wrecked our marriage and yet you *still* can't find the words to condemn him. There you were…*needing* me and he made sure that I was put out of the picture. How can you forgive that?'

Jaul swung impatiently away from her, his fierce loyalty to his late father strained by her candour. 'I must be honest with you. At that point in my recovery I didn't want to see you either. I did initially intend to visit you when I was stronger but by the time I was fit to see you so much time had passed that it seemed like a pointless exercise,' he divulged, tight-mouthed with restraint.

Inwardly Chrissie reeled as though he had struck her because that admission, that very dismissive terminology, was a body blow beyond her comprehension. 'I don't understand how you can say that it would have been pointless. How much time passed after the accident before you were fit to travel?' she demanded, folding her arms defensively as if she could hold in the emotions still churning inside her. His self-command, his granite-hard hold on control maddened her.

'It took well over a year for me even to get back on my feet again.' His lean dark features were taut and pale with the strain of being forced to recall that traumatic period of his life. 'My spine was damaged. It took further surgery and weeks of recovery before my doctors were able to estimate whether or not I could hope to walk again.'

In point of fact at a time when his whole world seemed to have fallen apart and he was confined to a hospital bed unable to move and requiring help for every little thing, Jaul had felt quite ridiculously unsurprised by the announcement that his new bride had run out on him as well. In truth he had been seriously depressed back then and traumatised by survivor's guilt because military friends and bodyguards he had known since childhood had died instantaneously in the same accident.

In addition to his deeply troubled state of mind and his belief that his father had bought Chrissie's loyalty

off, he had been painfully aware that he and Chrissie
had parted on very bad terms in Oxford. She'd been
angry with him for leaving her behind. In so many ways
back then Chrissie had been an idealistic dreamer and,
while he had loved those traits so very different from
his own, he had also seen them as a potential weakness
should life ever become tough. What could be tougher
for a youthful bride than a husband suddenly sentenced
to a wheelchair? Ultimately, his conviction that their
marriage was invalid as his father had asserted had
played the biggest role in his lack of action. After all,
if Chrissie wasn't even his wife what possible claim
could he have on her?

'But surely by that stage you must've had access to
a phone and to visitors and you could have contacted
me yourself?' Chrissie pressed accusingly.

Jaul's broad shoulders went rigid, his jawline squar-
ing at an aggressive slant. 'I was in a wheelchair…what
would I have said to you? I will be frank—I did not
want to approach you as a disabled man. You had accepted a five-million-pound settlement from my father
and I assumed that money was all you had ever really
wanted from me.'

Chrissie was outraged that Jaul had believed that
she had taken his father's money and run. Without a
doubt he had found that easier than confronting her
with his disability and the risk that he might not re-
gain the use of his legs. Jaul, the original action man
and macho to the core, was very physical in his tastes.
Deprived of his freedom of movement, forced to accept
such bodily weakness and restriction, how must he
have felt? But Chrissie suppressed that more empathetic
thought and tried to concentrate purely on facts. Jaul,

she realised with a sinking heart, had put his wretched pride first when he'd chosen not to approach her in a wheelchair and that truth hurt her more than anything else.

'But I didn't actually accept the money,' she whispered almost absently, so deep was her sense of rejection that he had found it impossible to reach out to her even when he was injured.

'You did.'

'No, I didn't. Your father left a bank draft for a ludicrous five million pounds on the table but I never cashed it.'

'But you said you had plenty of money when I first saw you again and naturally I *assumed*—'

'Only I wasn't referring to your father's bank draft,' Chrissie cut in ruefully. 'Cesare bought the Greek island which my sister and I had inherited from our mother. My share of the purchase price was very generous. I bought my apartment with some of it and put the rest into trust until my twenty-fifth birthday next year. That's what I meant about having plenty of money. I didn't touch a penny of your father's cash. I left that bank draft lying on the table.'

Jaul was transfixed by that claim. His keen gaze lowered, ebony brows drawing together in a frown. Five million pounds had impressed even him as an enormous sum to offer as a bribe to a young woman from an impoverished background. People lied, cheated and killed for far less money than Chrissie had been given. That was the main reason why he had never questioned his father's story but now he was determined to check out her story for himself. Could it be true that she had not claimed that money?

'When did my father's visit take place?' Jaul asked abruptly.

'About two months after you left and he was in a rage when I met him. You once told me he spoke English but he didn't use any within my hearing. His companion had to translate everything he said.'

'He had someone with him...aside of his body-guards?' Jaul shot the question at her in frowning surprise. 'Describe him.'

'Small, sixtyish, goatee beard and spectacles.'

Jaul fell very still as soon as he realised that there *was* a living witness to his father's meeting with his wife. 'My father's adviser, Yusuf,' he identified without hesitation, reflecting that Yusuf would be receiving a visit from him in the near future. Chrissie's allegations demanded and deserved closer scrutiny. If she hadn't taken the money, what had happened to it and why hadn't he been told? Keeping him unaware of the fact that his wife hadn't used the bank draft had ensured that he would misjudge her. It wasn't a thought that Jaul wanted to have but he knew that his father *must've* been informed that that bank draft had not been cashed.

Slowly, Chrissie settled down onto the sofa again, letting the fierce tension leach out of her spine. Her brain felt dazed as though she had gone ten punishing rounds with a boxer. Shock at what she had learned from Jaul was still passing through her in waves. Her bitterness and antagonism had been wrenched from her while she'd listened to the true story of what had separated them two years earlier. Jaul had *not* ditched her. Jaul had *not* voluntarily or cruelly chosen to desert her. In fact he had planned to return to her and, had fate not intervened with that accident and the lies his father had told to both of them, Jaul would almost certainly have returned to her.

For a split second she allowed herself to think of how that might have been and she swallowed painfully, struggling to imagine how she would've felt if Jaul had come back to her and if he had been with her when she'd discovered that she was pregnant. She realised that she was picturing an entirely different and infinitely happier world and fierce regret filled her, backed by a terrible anguished sense of loss because she was beginning to suspect that Jaul had been as miserable as she was when they were first separated. How *could* his father have believed he had the right to inflict such suffering on them both?

Hot, burning tears lashed the backs of Chrissie's eyes in an unsettling surge. She blinked rapidly, intense mortification threatening to engulf her because she only ever cried in the strictest privacy, a discipline learned the hard way after her life had fallen apart following Jaul's vanishing act two years earlier. She snatched in a deep, audible breath and Jaul swung away from the window, suppressing his uneasy thoughts at the prospect of confronting Yusuf, his late father's staunchest supporter.

Yusuf would not necessarily be discreet in the aftermath of such a discussion. It was a stark moment of choice for Jaul because he had to choose between his marriage and his respect for his father's memory. But he knew that that respect was not an excuse to avoid discovering an unpalatable truth. Yet if Chrissie *was* telling the truth, it would be an appalling truth that he would never be able to live with, he reflected grimly before swiftly suppressing that unproductive thought.

As he had been raised to do, he would do what he knew to be his duty and act with honour, regardless of what he found out.

'Where's the cloakroom?' Chrissie asked thickly, dragging his attention back to her.

When he saw the sheen in her turquoise eyes and the dampness on her cheeks, he tensed and took a sudden step forward.

'The first door at the top of the stairs but the bedroom en suites are closer,' Jaul volunteered, winged ebony brows pleating. 'You're upset…you're crying…'

Chrissie flew upright as though she were a puppet whose strings had been jerked without warning. 'Of course I'm not crying!' she protested huskily. 'It's stupid, it's just all this stuff about the past…it's confusing me.'

'I'm sorry,' Jaul breathed in a ragged undertone as he closed his arms round her slight, trembling figure to hold her still. 'I knew that telling you about the accident would rake it all up again, which was why I was so reluctant—'

'But I *had* to know the truth,' Chrissie told him, lifting her chin, an action that did nothing to hide the wet lustre of her eyes.

A tiny muscle pulled taut at the corner of his unsmiling mouth, his beautiful eyes flaring brilliant gold as he scored his knuckles lightly down the side of her face in a soothing gesture. 'I hurt you.'

Chrissie looked up at him and marvelled at how stunning he was even with his blue-black hair a little messy and his strong jawline stubbled. His black lashes were luxuriant above eyes of stormy gold. Wicked anticipation slid through her to create the kind of sudden tension that made her suck in her breath. As she connected with his burnished gaze a pulse was hammering like crazy above her collarbone. She wanted him to touch her so badly that her fingernails bit into her palms as her hands fisted. He was all lean muscle and potent strength as he eased her closer and her body thrummed, her blood racing like liquid lava through her veins. His warm, demanding mouth swooped down on hers and hot, blistering pleasure shot through her with the force of a lightning bolt.

Jaul lifted her up into his arms and carried her into the bedroom next door. As he settled her down on the bed her fingers feathered through his hair and instinctively closed into the silky black strands to hold him to her. 'Kiss me,' she told him, desperately needing to think of something…*anything* other than the reality that Jaul had almost died two years earlier. Had he died she would never have seen him again, never had the chance to hold him close and never had the joy of seeing him proudly hold his son in his arms.

CHAPTER EIGHT

JAUL KISSED MUCH as he made love, melding both passion and sleek proficiency into a devastating sensual assault.

Chrissie had been in emotional turmoil before he'd touched her and once that physical connection was made, she couldn't break it and she wrapped her arms round his neck, needing that security. Feverish kiss built on feverish kiss, stoking the fire flaming at the heart of her only to increase the ache there.

'If you let me have you now, I'll never let you go.' Jaul growled out that husky threat, staring down at her with compelling intensity. 'I can't fight the hunger you arouse in me.'

Chrissie gazed up at him and felt extraordinarily light-hearted for the first time since Jaul had come back into her life. He had not chosen to leave her: events had chosen for him. He had not condoned his father's interference and if he had been guilty of misjudging her on the question of that money, she needed to remember how newly married they had been and how vulnerable such ties could be in any untried relationship. Did she now punish him for his father's sins? Did she hold him to blame for having wanted to love and trust his only surviving parent? Although both Chrissie's parents had hurt her and held views contrary to her own, she had still loved them. She, more than anyone, should understand how basic and strong ran the need to love and trust a parent, she reasoned painfully. With a fingertip, she traced the fullness of his sensual lower lip and gloried in the stormy gold of his gaze, rejoicing in his innate passion.

'You don't have to fight it any more,' she told him softly.

'We're not going to rush this, *habibti*,' Jaul decreed, peeling off his shirt and depriving her of her breath in the same moment.

'*Rush...*' she urged, dry-mouthed, as he stripped with no more self-consciousness than a child. But then he didn't have a vain bone in his beautiful body, had absolutely no appreciation of the fact that he was a masculine work of art, a very aroused work of art, she recognised, her face warming as she momentarily stopped staring to kick off her shoes and run down the side zip on her dress. Jaul was all sleek, lean muscle, honed by exercise, lines indented across his six-pack, the vee at his hips rising out of the waistband of his boxers and dissected by the silky furrow of black hair that trailed down to the jutting hardness at his crotch.

'I rushed the last time...you walked out on me afterwards,' he reminded her wryly.

'But not because you were anything less than...er... perfect,' Chrissie framed in a rush of candour. 'But because I was all mixed up and I felt even worse after you presented me with that insane pre-nuptial contract I'd signed—'

'That's in the past...leave it there,' Jaul urged. 'We're making a new start.'

A new start. Disconcertingly, Chrissie found herself savouring that declaration. He didn't want the divorce. He wanted them to stay married and raise the children together. There was nothing wrong with that as an aspiration, was there? How could she fault him for that? If she let go of the past, could she too move forward into a more promising future? Why shouldn't she try? Why shouldn't she give their marriage another chance? What did she have to lose?

'A new start…?' she repeated unevenly.

'We're together again with our children. What could be more natural?' Jaul positively purred as he strolled towards the bed like a glossy prowling panther.

It did feel so natural to be with Jaul again, Chrissie acknowledged, studying his lean, extravagantly good-looking features while arrows of piercing heat surged through her in an intoxicating wave that left her boneless. No matter what he believed about her character, Jaul still wanted her, but then he had always wanted her and that was, at the very least, a foundation for the future.

Jaul feasted his eyes on her. 'Come here. We only have one more problem to solve. You're wearing far too many clothes,' he husked, sinking down on the bed and leaning closer to lift the hem of her dress and flip it deftly up over her head.

Chrissie emerged from the folds of the garment with luminous turquoise eyes, wide and bright against her flushed complexion. He unclasped her bra and tossed it aside. 'I want to look at you.'

Her breathing rupturing in her throat, Chrissie fought an instinctive urge to cover herself and her colour heightened as she leant back against the pillows.

Jaul curved reverent hands over the pouting swell of her breasts. 'Pure perfection,' he murmured thickly.

He tugged at the pale pink straining buds and then, emitting a groan of surrender, he lowered his head and hungrily enveloped them in his mouth. It felt so good to Chrissie that she gasped and clutched at his luxuriant black hair. Her whole body was coming alive and singing and the blaze he was awakening at the heart of her was burning fever bright, her lower limbs moving restively, her thighs pressing together on the hollow ache he had roused. At that moment, she had never wanted anything more than she wanted his touch and she shifted her hips, edgy and needy, before her hands began to explore him, reacquainting herself with the corrugated flatness of his abdomen before stroking down to the long, thick prominence of his erection. He was smooth as silk, hard as steel.

'Stop. I'm too excited,' Jaul warned her raggedly. 'I want to come inside you.'

'*Rush,*' she told him again with greater urgency, twitching her hips upwards again while grazing her fingertips teasingly over the crown of his manhood.

'You don't tell me what to do in bed,' Jaul husked.

With a lightness of heart she hadn't experienced in a very long time, Chrissie laughed out loud. 'Lie back for me for just five minutes…and I promise you, you'll do whatever I want,' she whispered provocatively.

'Not tonight.'

His hand skimmed down over her tummy and between her slender thighs. A fingertip traced the wet, silky entrance to her body and her hips jackknifed, hunger rising so swiftly and powerfully that she almost cried out.

Jaul shifted down the bed and found her damp, heated core with his tongue and this time she did cry out, her breathing fractured, her throat convulsing as the incredible pleasure blasted her into another reality where blissful ripples of sensation engulfed her, locking out absolutely everything else. Her head twisted back and forth on the pillow, perspiration breaking on her skin, her nipples peaking as his fingers delved deep into her and his talented tongue tormented her into ecstasy. The climax hit her like a speeding train, snatching her up and throwing her high.

'That was…amazing,' Chrissie mumbled weakly, the words slurring as he lifted her up and flipped her over to settle her down on her knees.

'I aim to please, *habibti.*'

Having positioned her on the bed to his satisfaction, Jaul drove into her tight, wet channel and the sensation of being stretched to the utmost was so irresistibly seductive that a strangled sob of encouragement escaped Chrissie. She was out of control and revelling in the awareness. A frenzy of need gripped her as he surged and ebbed inside her sensitive sheath. With every plunging entrance, her heart slammed against her ribcage and her excitement climbed another notch. He ground his body into hers and then ratcheted up the tempo with long, smooth, deep thrusts until she was literally sobbing out loud with tormented pleasure. Her spine arching, she pushed back against him, guided by an impatient frantic need she could not withstand. As that reached a peak, she went careening over the crest into an orgasm that flooded her with joy, satisfaction and warmth and listened to Jaul groan out loud in completion.

'Now *that* was truly worthy of the word *amazing*,' Jaul rasped as he turned her back over and dragged her back into the hot, damp embrace of his lean, powerful body.

He had both arms anchored round her, imprisoning her as though at any moment she might make a break for freedom. But Chrissie was exactly where she wanted to be. Strong emotions were still churning round inside her. Jaul had said that hoping was not a sin and here she was caught up in hoping too, she acknowledged ruefully. For the first time she understood herself: she still loved Jaul and in admitting that she was shedding the heavy burden of past memories and disillusionment to focus on the new start he had promised.

'So…er…you mentioned another wedding,' she reminded him gently.

'If you think you could bear it,' Jaul murmured cautiously, tensing as she buried her head below his chin, wondering whether she was driven by affection or avoidance.

'I think I could, particularly if it was more like the dream wedding I never got,' she confided softly.

'The dream wedding?' he prompted blankly.

'Because you didn't want us to attract too much attention I wore a plain black dress at the embassy do,' she reminded him. 'This time around I'd like a proper wedding gown…and, oh, yes, I want my sister to come over for it.'

'That could all be arranged. Western wedding gowns are very popular here.'

'Seriously?' Chrissie looked up at him with surprised turquoise eyes.

The sudden charismatic grin Chrissie had almost

forgotten flashed across his lean dark features. 'Seriously…but it will have to be a rush job. My advisers are hoping we can stage this the day after tomorrow—'

'The day after tomorrow?' she yelped in disbelief, pulling free of him to scramble out of bed naked. 'I need to phone Lizzie and warn her!'

Pleasantly surprised at the ease with which she had given her agreement, Jaul rose at a more leisurely pace. He laughed as he listened to Chrissie chattering to her sister on the phone line in the next room and even paused for thirty seconds to appreciate the picture his wife made standing there stark naked, her slender, graceful figure gleaming porcelain pale and pink in the sunlit room. Concerned that one of the staff might enter without offering sufficient warning, he fetched a towelling robe from the bathroom and held it out while Chrissie dug her arms into it with a lingering smile in her eyes that held his attention like a magnet. He strode back into the bedroom and dug his mobile phone out of his jacket to call Yusuf.

But his father's former aide was unavailable. Yusuf's manservant informed Jaul that his employer was in the USA visiting his daughter and that it would be two weeks before he was home again. Jaul grimaced, knowing it would be inappropriate to try and tackle such a controversial subject with Yusuf over the phone. He had no choice but to await the older man's return. And while he waited, more and more questions and inconsistencies would pile up in the back of his mind. Even worse, he acknowledged with sudden grim awareness, if Chrissie proved to be telling the truth without exaggeration on all counts, *he* would suddenly be the guilty party, who had virtually destroyed her life, and how could he ever live with that conclusion?

Chrissie put the phone down and breathed in deep, astonished to recognise that she had been gabbling to her sister like an overexcited teenager. As she asked herself what had come over her, she lodged by the window, which was bounded by a stone balcony and a glorious view of the trees flourishing in the garden below. Was she a total idiot? she was suddenly demanding of herself. She was still in love with Jaul and she wanted to give their marriage the best possible chance to thrive that she could...*but*.

And it was a very large 'but'; she had to be realistic and stop behaving like a dizzy adolescent. She needed to view their situation as it was and not wrap it up in fancy trappings, for the surest way to a failed marriage would be setting out with too high expectations only to be rewarded with a slow, steady process of disenchantment.

Jaul wasn't in love with her. Sexual chemistry wasn't love even though the powerful attraction that had first drawn them together was still red hot. Other facts spoke too loud to be ignored, however, she reflected unhappily. Jaul had come to London to see her in the first place because he'd wanted a divorce and he had only changed his mind about that *after* he'd realised that he was a father.

He only wanted to stay married to Chrissie now because she was the mother of his children and Tarif was the heir to his throne. Love and affection had nothing to do with that decision. Jaul was prepared to behave as a husband and father, not only to meet the conservative expectations of his people, but also to provide the twins with a stable and respectable home background. It was a praiseworthy motivation but it did not mean that Jaul was *happy* about embracing Chrissie as his wife and queen or that he would willingly have selected her for that role now.

After all, what choice had Jaul had? His passionate temperament was uniquely misleading. He was a wildly passionate male but, at heart, he was ruled by cool intellect and practicality. The marriage he had chosen to put behind him and dismiss had come back to haunt him in the worst way and now he was trapped with a wife he couldn't divorce without shocking and disappointing his people. Fate could well be forcing him to make the best of a bad situation. Her skin turned clammy while she pondered that humiliating theory but she knew that it would be stupid to ignore that wounding analysis of their marriage and even stupider to assume that sharing Jaul's bed meant anything more to him than the casual and convenient slaking of sexual need. Sobered by those reflections, Chrissie tightened the sash on the oversized robe and went back into the bedroom, relieved to appreciate that there were two en suites attached to it. Just at that moment she needed her own space and peace in which to rebuild her poise. Home truths, she thought reluctantly, were necessary to keep her feet on the ground but, my goodness, they could *hurt*…

CHAPTER NINE

WITH LIZZIE BY her side, Chrissie crossed the entrance hall of the British Embassy in Marwan City with her pale head held high, her hair swept up and ornamented only with a short veil and her perilously high sparkly shoes tap-tapping on the tiles.

Her dress was such a neat fit that she could barely breathe in it but she felt like ten million dollars in the exquisite dress with its shimmering embroidered fabric glistening even in the dulled light. She was a stock size...*just*, and Zaliha had discovered that several exclusive designers were willing to fly in a selection of dresses and accessories for a queen's approval. The gown hugged her arms and her upper body, nipping in at the waist before flaring out with the fluidity of the most expensive silk.

'You look spectacular,' her sister whispered with fierce pride. 'And I'm so pleased that Jaul is making such an effort to give your marriage a firmer footing in the present.'

If anything, Chrissie's smile dimmed as she had not allowed it to dim during the lengthy photographic session that had preceded her departure from the royal palace. Lizzie had not recognised that Chrissie was fulfilling a more public than private role in agreeing to the renewing of her wedding vows. Chrissie, conversely, was hugely aware that a visible wedding was very much what the people of Marwan wanted to see and rejoice in. The first half of the day would celebrate her British identity with the blessing at the embassy followed by a formal wedding breakfast back at the palace. But afternoon would find Chrissie being prepared for a traditional Marwani wedding, which would be staged at the palace at dusk and followed by a big party.

Jaul broke off his conversation with his brother-in-law, Cesare, to focus on his bride's entrance with dark eyes that swiftly turned to scorching gold. She was so beautiful in that gloriously feminine gown. For the first time he appreciated what the hole-and-corner wedding he had insisted on in London two years earlier had cost her. That had been no dream day for a starry-eyed bride, he conceded remorsefully. He had wanted to present his father with a fait accompli but marrying Chrissie in the bright spotlight of paparazzi publicity would only have made his father more bitter and hostile. In the end, though, his attempt not to rebel too publicly against his father's edicts had only exacerbated the situation and had ensured that their marriage remained a dangerous secret.

As the embassy chaplain approached her, Chrissie could barely drag her eyes from Jaul's strikingly handsome dark features. His lean, powerful physique sheathed in a light grey morning suit, Jaul was drop-dead gorgeous, but Chrissie had been even more taken with him when she had seen him wearing jeans at dawn to get down on the floor of the nursery and play with Tarif and Soraya before he began his working day. The twins chattered with excitement when their father appeared now, associating his frequent visits with the kind of fun rough-and-tumble games they adored. Watching Jaul play with their children warmed the cold spot deep inside Chrissie, which repeatedly sought to warn her that if she wasn't careful she would get her heart broken again.

Jaul reached for her hand as the chaplain began to speak and Chrissie suppressed the treacherous swell of her insecurity. For a few seconds indeed, she was lost in the memory of their wedding day two years previously and of the joyful sense of security she had experienced as that ring went on her finger, a security that had proved to be sadly short-lived. Her rings were back where they belonged now because she had reclaimed them from Cesare's safe.

Chrissie smiled, reminding herself that they were making a fresh start at being together and that, so far, Jaul was doing absolutely everything right. She didn't *need* his love and devotion, she told herself impatiently. She would focus her energies on becoming the very best mother and Queen she could be, not on chasing soap-bubble dreams of romance. He had been her first love, for goodness' sake, and they had only been students. That time couldn't be reclaimed or relived and, anyway, would she even *want* to go back there? Back to the silly rows they had once had, rows redolent of their immaturity and inability to compromise?

One thing she did appreciate was that Jaul had changed. She wondered if what he had endured in the wake of the accident had made that change in him because he was considerably more tolerant and less domineering than she remembered him being.

More cameras flashed as Jaul escorted her out of the function room. In the limousine on the way back to the palace, he flashed her a charismatic smile and lifted a lean brown hand to acknowledge the crowds lining the side of the road. 'One down, only one more to go. We will feel very much married by the end of this day.'

Her turquoise eyes brightened with amusement. 'Yes…'

'Tonight we'll be travelling into the desert for a few days. I have to meet with the tribal sheikhs and it's the perfect opportunity to introduce you to their families. While we are becoming an increasingly urban society, there is not a family in the country that does not have a connection by birth or marriage to one of the tribes. Their support is influential,' he told her quietly. 'Zaliha will travel with us as an interpreter for your benefit.'

'Of course. I'll have to get lessons in Arabic.'

'It wouldn't be of much use to you in the desert. The tribes speak an ancient dialect,' Jaul told her ruefully and reached for her hand, disconcerting her. 'I really do appreciate your can-do attitude to all of this.'

'I'll do whatever I have to do to be a good queen,' Chrissie assured him, lifting her chin. 'I'm not planning to embarrass you or the children either now or in the future.'

His luxuriant black lashes lowered over a brightly assessing gleam of gold. 'A commendable goal but I have a rather more personal outlook.'

Chrissie tugged her fingers free lightly. 'Have you really?' she dared before she could bite back that cynical challenge. 'I doubt very much that you see our marriage in personal terms. How could you? The ceremonies today are the ultimate publicity blitz calculated to please your subjects.'

'What we appear to feel in public can continue in private. It doesn't have to be fake,' Jaul countered smoothly.

'Let's keep it simple, Jaul. We'll both do our best in our respective roles and see how it goes,' she suggested lightly.

'As you wish.' Jaul wondered what had happened to the outspoken and passionate young woman he had married. That Chrissie would never have settled for such prosaic goals. No, indeed she would have demanded his love and attention and shouted loudly if she failed to receive her due. Was the change in her the result of his apparent desertion and the struggles of single parenthood? Ultimately was he to blame? The thought appalled him.

Back at the palace a European-style meal was served. Tarif and Soraya joined the table in their high chairs and ate at speed before demanding the freedom of the floor, whereupon they made complete nuisances of themselves crawling below the table and tugging at shoelaces and trouser legs. Highly amused, Jaul hauled Tarif out from below the tablecloth and returned him to his nanny. Soraya was curled up sleepily on her mother's lap, forcing Chrissie to dip into her dessert with one hand. Zaliha gave her a nod when it was time for her to go off and prepare for her second wedding. Passing Soraya to the nursemaid hovering expectantly behind her chair and closely followed by Lizzie, Chrissie left the table.

Zaliha introduced Chrissie to the crowd of older women waiting in the bedroom suite, which had been set aside for the wedding preparations. Every tribe had put forward a representative to help dress the Queen. Chrissie removed her wedding gown and entered the bathroom, an old-fashioned one with a giant, sunken tiled tub that had evidently escaped Jaul's improvements. The water in the tub was awash with rose petals and some highly fragrant herbal concoction. A basin was brought to help in the washing of her hair.

'It must be done five times,' Zaliha explained in an undertone. 'Nobody knows why but it has always been done this way.'

Lizzie grinned and parked herself down on the chair provided for her. 'I'm going to enjoy every minute of watching this process,' she forecast cheerfully. 'It's so wonderfully exotic.'

Chrissie bathed and lay back while her hair was soaked in scented oil and rinsed over and over again. She emerged from the bath swathed in a big towel and climbed straight onto a massage table, where she was expertly kneaded and moisturised while at the same time an artist drew swirling, elaborate henna patterns on the backs of her hands and on her feet. The painstaking care with which every strand of her hair and every inch of her skin were anointed with some special preparation was amazingly relaxing and at one stage she dozed off for a little while, only wakening when she was forced to do so by the woman trilling in the bedroom.

'They chant for your good luck and fertility,' Zaliha explained. 'You're already a step ahead there with twins...'

While her hair was dried into a shining white-blonde sheet of silk falling down her back, make-up was applied. Zaliha passed her a turquoise silk beaded top and matching long skirt while ethnic turquoise and silver jewellery was tumbled out from a big casket onto the dressing table and picked through. A headdress of beaten silver coins was attached to her brow.

'You look like a Viking warrior princess,' Lizzie whispered teasingly. 'Jaul will love it.'

The whole regalia felt like fancy dress to Chrissie but she wore it with pride, knowing that the outfit she wore and the respect she was clearly demonstrating for Marwani traditions would please many people. Marwan was a rapidly changing society, keen to move forward into the modern technological world but afraid of losing its culture in the process. Professional photographs were taken with great care in the room next door and then she was led downstairs for the ceremony.

Jaul had been enjoying much more relaxed preparations, which consisted merely of a shower, a change of clothing and prayers with the imam before he joined the retinue of VIPs and personal staff awaiting him.

Jaul saw Chrissie the minute he entered the room. In Marwani costume, she was the very image of a perfect porcelain doll but a breathtakingly beautiful one. His body reacted more like an adolescent boy's than an adult's. Instantly he turned his head away again, blocking her out, willing back his vanquished control with the grim awareness that no woman had ever affected him the way she did. But then she was the only woman he had ever loved and nothing had ever hurt as much as the loss of her. He had closed off those emotions inside him, never to revisit them. Hadn't that been the healthy response to that much pain?

'Your wife is even more lovely in person than she is in photos, Your Majesty,' the elderly sheikh by his side remarked, shooting him out of introspection into looking at Chrissie again. 'You are a very fortunate man.'

Was it good fortune to have had her and lost her again? To have been forced to blackmail her with their children to win her back again? As his conscience bit into him Jaul thought not. He had put his children's needs first, he reminded himself doggedly, ensuring that, unlike him who had lost his mother at birth, Tarif and Soraya would grow up with their mother loving and supporting them. But what if ultimately what he offered was not enough to keep Chrissie with him? A hollow expanded inside his chest at the prospect of losing her again. The answer was simple, he acknowledged grittily. He had to make very, very sure that Chrissie *wanted* to stay with him.

Chrissie's gaze flashed round the room before arrowing back to identify Jaul. It was the first time she had seen him clad in traditional clothing. A gold-edged black cloak flowing back over his broad shoulders, Jaul wore beige linen with a pristine white buttoned undershirt, the pale colour amplifying his bronzed skin. A headdress bound with gold cord covered his black hair and mysteriously contrived to enhance the flawless cut of his spectacular bone structure, highlighting the spiky ebony lashes rimming his lustrous dark eyes and the clean, sculpted beauty of his wide, sensual lips. He looked both exotic and sleekly, darkly beautiful. She sucked in a steadying breath.

'Jaul's a bit like Cesare. It doesn't matter what you dress him in,' Lizzie whispered teasingly in her ear. 'He will always look hot.'

The wedding ceremony was formal and brief. Their hands were ritually bound together and then released again. The more light-hearted aspect of their renewal of their vows at the British Embassy was replaced by a tone of gravity as prayers were chanted. A little intimidated by the solemnity of the occasion, Chrissie turned back to face Jaul, needing reassurance. He cupped her elbow, very much aware that their every move was still under scrutiny and that any public demonstration of intimacy would be unacceptable.

'All done,' he said quietly as if she were a child who had survived having a plaster ripped off a grazed knee.

Night had fallen while they were indoors. In the palace's largest courtyard, braziers burned and colourful lights illuminated the palm trees and shrubs against the darkness. Jaul guided Chrissie to one of a pair of gilded thrones set centrally while all around them staff hurried back and forth with trays of lightly steaming food.

'I will serve you,' Jaul declared, waving away the servant eager to wait on them with a determined hand and approaching a laden table to lift a plate.

He was deep in thought. The wedding staged here in the home of his ancestors had touched him deeply. Chrissie was his wife and it was his duty to protect her, a duty he had failed in when he had first married her. While the accident had not been his fault and he could not have avoided it, he knew he had let her down. A man who took on the responsibility of a wife should always make provision for his wife's safety and security in the event of a tragedy, he reasoned guiltily. He had been young and irresponsible and thoughtless and she had paid the price for his arrogance. But he would ensure that she had no further cause to regret their marriage.

Chrissie was painfully aware of their guests watching as Jaul served her with food.

'In seeing to your needs before his own, the King shows you great honour,' Zaliha explained as a maid served them with glasses of juice.

The music began. Dancers put on an exhibition of acrobatic athleticism. Poetry was recited. Good wishes were tendered. A comedian performed a skit but, even with Jaul's translation, Chrissie didn't get the jokes. Cameras gleamed and whirred in the bright lights, quietly recording everything. As the night air grew chillier and gooseflesh prickled below the sleeves of Chrissie's light top, Jaul raised her up and dropped his cloak round her slim shoulders. 'It is time for us to leave.'

A convoy of four-wheel-drive vehicles awaited them outside. Chrissie climbed into the lead vehicle and watched as Jaul's bodyguards divided to fill the vehicles behind. Her brow indented. 'What happened to your old bodyguards?'

And she knew the instant she saw the pallor leach away his natural colour and his haunted eyes met hers that she need not have asked. 'The accident?' she whispered in distress, involuntarily recalling Hakim, the tall, thin, serious one and his younger brother, Altair, who had always had a smile on his face.

Jaul nodded in silent acknowledgement and regret.

Chrissie reached for his hand and squeezed it. 'I'm so sorry,' she said frankly, painfully aware that Jaul had grown up with the two brothers.

The convoy rocked noisily along a rough track into the desert. Chrissie almost tumbled off the seat several times until Jaul secured her with a protective arm. 'Have we far to go?' she asked, certain her teeth were going to rattle right out of her head with the jolts and bumps.

'We are almost there. We pitched the camp closer than usual to the palace.'

Jaul stepped out into the dense shadow cast by a huge tent while lights flared both outside it and within it. 'We will have every comfort here,' he assured her, helping her out. 'The twins will join us tomorrow. It would not have made sense to disrupt their sleep.'

The tent was in no shape or form what she had expected. For a start it was much more spacious than she had foreseen and partitioned off into different sections. The seating area was in the front portion and clearly for entertaining. The walls were hung with bead and wool work while the floor was covered with an exquisite rug and fur and silk throws and elaborate soft cushions provided an opulent accent to the seating. 'Wow...this is not camping as I imagined it.'

'We're not camping. Are you hungry?' Jaul enquired, thrusting open a door hidden by a hanging.

'No, I'm absolutely stuffed,' Chrissie admitted, following him into a bedroom even more magnificently decorated than the entertainment area. 'No stinting on comforts here...'

'But we will have to share a bathroom,' Jaul confided, casting open another concealed door to let her see the facilities. 'We will be as comfortable here as we would be at the palace. For generations my forebears have visited the desert in spring and late summer to meet with the tribal elders.'

Glancing in a mirror, Chrissie removed the coin headdress because, like the rest of the handmade antique jewellery she wore, it was very heavy. Stilling behind her in silence, Jaul undid the clasp of the necklace she wore without being asked and she caught it as it slid down and settled it on the mirror tray before pushing back her hair to detach the earrings.

'Which outfit did you prefer?' she suddenly asked him. 'The wedding gown or *this*…?'

'You looked fantastic in the white gown, like a model on a catwalk. But my heart *raced* when I saw you in this…' He smoothed long brown fingers over a slender shoulder. 'The colour reflects the shade of your eyes and your glorious curves are only hinted at, which I liked,' he confided huskily. 'Perhaps I am more like my ancestors than I ever dreamt and a hundred years ago I would have veiled you from all eyes but my own…'

Warmth flared in her cheeks. She had expected him to tell her that he preferred her in the wedding gown and he had surprised her with an honesty that she found extraordinarily sexy. 'Veiled?' she teased.

'Your beauty could blind a man,' Jaul husked, trailing his warm mouth across the pale skin of her shoulder and drawing her back against him. 'You blinded me the first moment I saw you but it was the wrong time in the wrong place and in the wrong company.'

'Yes,' she acknowledged, breasts swelling from the proximity of his hands and a very basic need to be touched as her breath feathered in her throat.

Yet his allusion to the discomfiture of their first meeting surprised her, for nothing could have been more awkward than encountering him fresh from bedding her friend and flatmate the night before. Even though her friend had swiftly moved on to another man and indeed moved in with him, that unhappy connection had ensured Chrissie resisted Jaul's advances.

His lips caressed her throat as he drew her down on the bed and as a shiver of almost painful sexual awareness travelled through her she blinked as he lifted her hand, splayed her fingers and smoothly threaded a ring onto her wedding finger.

'What's this?' she gasped, scanning the band of incredibly glittery gems now set next to her wedding ring. *'Pink?'*

'Pink diamonds. A gift as flawless as you. My wedding gift.'

'I never even thought of giving you a gift!' she exclaimed with a groan of frustration.

'But you gave me Tarif and Soraya, whose worth is beyond price,' Jaul declared without hesitation. 'I can never thank you enough for our children.'

Her eyes shone luminous in the lamplight because she realised he was sincere. Her fingers shifted on the sheet beneath her hand and she frowned, glancing down to see that the bed had been sprinkled with silky pink rose petals. 'Are these supposed to be a fertility aid or something?' she asked suspiciously.

'Roses have always been revered in our climate. The Marwan press has already christened you "*Our* English Rose".'

Chrissie laughed and rolled her eyes.

'It is true. You are very beautiful.'

Encountering the lustrous glint of gold in Jaul's dark deep-set eyes, Chrissie flushed because a tiny ball of heat was suddenly igniting deep down inside her. The wild potency of his compelling sexuality made her mouth run dry and her heart pound. It had always been like that: one look from Jaul ensnared her.

Long fingers curving to her cheekbone, he melded his mouth with hot, fierce pleasure to the lush softness of hers. As he licked along the sealed seam of her lips, it was like a lightning strike with electricity snaking through every fibre of Chrissie's body. Something clenched low in her pelvis, an ache stirring wanton warmth and dampness between her thighs.

'Jaul…' she whispered shakily between reddened lips.

'Very beautiful…and finally mine,' Jaul growled, peeling off his headdress and hauling her onto his lap to embark on the tiny pearl buttons running down the back of her top.

'Very much married anyway,' she mumbled, her body taking fire at the mere thought of his touch. 'That's married three times over now. There'll be no denying that.'

'I will never deny you again, *habibti*,' Jaul muttered raggedly, closing his hands round the firm swell of her unbound breasts, his fingers tugging at the straining tips before he rolled her back onto the bed. With deft ease, he tugged off her skirt and underwear and knelt down to slip off her shoes.

Chrissie watched him strip and leave everything in a messy heap. His untidiness, the result of never ever having to clear up after himself, had once infuriated her, but now it struck a familiar note that gave her lips a wry curve. His lithe, lean bronzed body was fully, unashamedly aroused. His eyes burned gold with potent hunger below languorously lowered black lashes. 'I want you so much…'

Chrissie lay across the bed feeling as wondrously seductive as Cleopatra, for the first time ever unconcerned by her nakedness. The intensity of Jaul's desire had always enthralled her. She was not perfect, she *knew* she was not perfect but Jaul had always vehemently disagreed. There had never been anyone else for her purely because only Jaul made her burn with earthy longing and only Jaul could look at her as though she were a goddess come to earth in human flesh. He slid down beside her, his stunning eyes all hot intensity as he claimed her mouth again with devouring hunger. She shifted fluidly under him, her thighs sliding apart, her legs curving up round his hips to bring the most needy part of her into line with his arousal.

'You're trying to hurry me again,' Jaul censured. 'This is a special night.'

'Every night with you is special,' Chrissie broke in, tilting up to him, inviting him into her with every weapon in her feminine armoury.

He pulled back from her briefly to reach for a condom and returned to stroke the heated damp flesh between her thighs, teasing her in ways that made her writhe and jerk with a readiness she couldn't conceal. When he finally thrust into her, she expelled her breath in a joyous hiss of sensual shock and pleasure and flung her head back. *'Yes!'* she gasped.

Jaul withdrew and glided into her again and her inner muscles clenched tight around him. With his every carnal thrust, excitement leapt higher, perspiration beading on her skin as her heart hammered. He pushed her back against the pillows, lifting her legs over his shoulders to gain better access to her willing body.

'You're a total minx, you scramble my wits,' he told her raggedly, his control breaking as she lifted her hips to deepen his penetration and his pace quickening to a more forceful rhythm.

And then there was nothing but the passion and the wild, crazy excitement he induced until she felt as though she were about to fly clean out of her skin. Molten heat consumed her as he pounded into her with fierce hunger and when the finish came it was spectacular for both of them and a blaze of ecstasy that was overwhelming.

Chrissie lay with her cheek pressed up against Jaul's shoulder. 'I have to learn to trust you again,' she mused, speaking her thoughts out loud because all barriers were down. 'I know—intellectually speaking—that you didn't *choose* to desert me but I've always had a hard time trusting men.'

Jaul smoothed her tossed hair. 'Why?'

'Mum lived with a lot of loser men while I was growing up,' she told him ruefully. 'Either they were drunks or gamblers or they stole her money or beat her up.'

Jaul was shocked, belatedly registering that Chrissie had always been cagey about her background and only now was he understanding why. 'That does explain some things about you. You were always so suspicious of me, always expecting the worst.'

'Mum married her last partner and he was the worst of all...' she admitted heavily.

'In what way?' Jaul prompted.

'It's sordid,' she mumbled, abruptly pulling away from him.

Jaul hauled her back into his arms without hesitation. 'There should be nothing you can't tell me. Your mother's mistakes are not your mistakes and I will not judge you by them.'

Chrissie swivelled round in the circle of his arms. 'Before Mum died, my stepfather was making her work as a prostitute,' she framed sickly. 'Men would come to the house during the day. Lizzie doesn't know about it because she was at secondary and she had a job after school but I was only seven and home at lunchtime. Once I went upstairs to the bathroom and I saw Mum in bed with a man and there was a huge row.'

Jaul tipped up her face, seeing the distance and defensiveness etched in her turquoise eyes. 'What happened?'

'My stepfather hit me. I was much older before I understood what was going on. After that I was locked in my room every day after school… I was very scared of my stepfather.'

'I am so very sorry you had to go through that,' Jaul breathed in a raw, driven undertone, wishing he could look up the stepfather and kill him for terrorising the sensitive, innocent child Chrissie had once been. 'But it is not your disgrace to bear.'

'It's never felt like that, though,' Chrissie confided, willing to meet his beautiful eyes again, anxiously in search of any sign of revulsion in his gaze and relieved to see only concern etched there. 'Now tell me something you're ashamed of…' she invited to distract him from asking further questions.

Not checking out his father's story about her once he was fit to do so.

But Jaul didn't want to rake up that divisive past and instead presented her with another less than stellar moment. 'I lost my virginity with a very high-class hooker in Dubai,' he told her grimly. 'Believe me, I was of an age where it was past time I found out what sex was like.'

'Why was that?' she asked curiously.

'The first real freedom I had ever had was when I went to university in the UK,' Jaul confided with a grimace. 'I had no experience whatsoever of normal life.'

Chrissie rested her head down on his shoulder and studied him with drowsy turquoise eyes of sympathy while thinking of how badly she had misunderstood him when she'd first met him and assumed he was the quintessential Arab playboy. In truth he had spent his youthful years of supposed irresponsibility in boarding school and the army with even his free time mapped out by his controlling father. If he had gone a little wild when he'd first slipped that leash, she was sure only a saint could blame him for it.

It dismayed her to appreciate how little they had actually known about each other when they had first married, but it soothed her that she understood him better now and could accept that in possession of his faculties and the true facts he would never have abandoned her.

Bandar greeted Jaul over his morning coffee by the fire the following morning.

His aide gave him a list of the day's events and passed on urgent messages before pausing to extend an envelope. 'This arrived in the diplomatic bag yesterday. It's from Yusuf and apparently it's personal and confidential.' Bandar raised his brows at that surprising label being applied to any item sent by as aloof a personality as his former boss.

Jaul stiffened and lost colour before grasping the envelope. As soon as he was alone, he tore it open. Somewhere in the depths of the tent he could hear Chrissie singing tunelessly in the shower but, for once, he failed to smile. He was reading what his father's former adviser had to say and in the short note of fervent apology one sentence stood out clearer than any other.

Bearing in mind my actions two years ago, it would have been an offence for me to enter the same room as your queen and offer my best wishes on the occasion of your wedding.

And there it was in a handful of words: what Jaul had most feared. It was confirmation of everything Chrissie had told him because it was obvious that Yusuf had felt too ashamed of his treatment of Chrissie in the past to attend their wedding. That confirmation struck Jaul like a body blow. His stomach lurched and he sprang to his feet, too unsettled to sit still. Evidently, everything Chrissie had told him was the truth. She *had* been thrown out of his Oxford apartment and humiliated. She *had* gone to the Marwani Embassy in London to enquire about her missing husband, only for those visits to be mocked and hushed up. She had *not* accepted money from his father.

Jaul had nourished a secret hope that Chrissie could be exaggerating her experiences after his disappearance, that perhaps what she had endured was not quite as traumatic as she had made it sound, but Yusuf's reaction to Chrissie's reappearance in Jaul's life as his queen was uniquely revealing. Jaul still wanted to hear the details of Yusuf's dealings with his wife on King Lut's behalf but he would wait until the older man returned to Marwan to receive them. After all, he already knew the most crucial facts, he reminded himself heavily. His wife had told him how she had suffered and he had doubted her every word, had literally prayed that her lively imagination had encouraged her to embellish her story. And wasn't this his due reward for his lack of faith in his wife and his all-consuming loyalty to his father's memory? What had happened to his loyalty to the woman he had married?

Self-evidently, his father had lied to him shamelessly over and over again. Lut clearly hadn't cared what he'd had to say or do to destroy his son's marriage. Jaul was appalled that the man he had respected and cared for could have gone to such brutally selfish lengths to deprive his son of the woman he loved.

As the sun began to climb higher in the sky, driving off the early morning chill, Jaul paced the sand, oblivious to the anxious watch of his guards. He could not escape certain devastating conclusions: he had virtually wrecked Chrissie's life and, worst of all, he had not just done it once, he had done it *twice*. The first time he had married her and left her pregnant and without support and the second time he had blackmailed her into moving to Marwan and giving their marriage a second chance. How did any man come back from such grievous mistakes? What right did he have to try and hold onto a woman he knew he didn't deserve?

While being angry and hostile at the outset, Chrissie had come round sufficiently to offer him a measure of forgiveness and understanding. But she didn't owe him either, did she? He had done nothing to earn her forgiveness. An honourable man would let her go free, Jaul reckoned, perspiration dampening his lean dark features in the heat of the sun. An honourable man would instantly own up to his mistakes and give her the freedom to make a choice about whether she wanted to stay or go…

It was the most humiliating moment to discover that he was evidently *not* an honourable man, for the prospect of facing life without Chrissie and the twins by his side was not one that Jaul could bring himself to even contemplate.

He had screwed up, he had screwed up so badly, he reasoned fiercely, that he could only do better in the future. But the shame of his misjudgement felt like a giant rock lodged in his chest. He watched Chrissie curl up on a seat in the shade while fruit and rolls were brought to her for breakfast. Her shining hair was loose round her lovely face and she wore not a scrap of make-up, her slender body fetchingly clad in khaki capris and a plain white tee. She was his wife…but for how much longer? Stress locked tight every muscle in his lithe, powerful body.

CHAPTER TEN

'WHAT HAPPENED TO that horse you idolised?' Jaul asked lazily.

'Hero's in a sanctuary close to the farm where I used to live with Dad,' Chrissie told him as they rode back to the oasis encampment with the sun slowly rising to chase the coolness from the sky. Her eyes were wide and bright, appreciative of the surprising and colourful beauty of the barren landscape at dawn. 'I'm afraid I haven't seen him in months. While I was working and looking after the twins, it was just impossible to get up there for a visit but maybe next time we're in London I could make a special trip to see him.'

'Why's your horse in a sanctuary?' Jaul pressed with obvious incomprehension.

'Because, Mr Spoilt-Rotten-Rich, when my father had to vacate the farm tenancy I no longer had any-where to house Hero and no money to pay for his up-keep either. Then, luckily for me, we sold the island to Cesare and I gave the sanctuary an endowment to give Hero a home for life,' Chrissie explained without heat as she gently stroked the neck of the beautiful Arabian mare she was riding. 'He's safe, well-looked-after and happy. It was the best I could do for him.'

Their time in the desert was almost over, Chrissie reflected, for they were travelling back to the palace as soon as they returned to the camp. The palace stables were packed with wonderful horse flesh and Jaul had had his stallion and her gorgeous high-stepping mare brought out for their use. Every day they had gone riding at dawn and at dusk when the desert heat was at its coolest. She had adored those quiet times with Jaul and the knowledge that their mutual love of horses and fresh-air activity was something they could share. But although Jaul had been endlessly attentive and reassuring she could not escape the suspicion that something was amiss with him.

While Jaul had endured long meetings with the tribal sheikhs, who had arrived every morning to speak with him and stayed throughout the day, Chrissie had spent the time with their wives and families. She enjoyed meeting people and learning about their lives and with Zaliha to translate she had held story-telling sessions with the children and all formality had been abandoned while she entertained them. Jaul had called those sessions an 'unqualified success' and had complimented her on her easy manner with his people. He had even asked her to consider working with the professionals on a nursery education development programme for Marwan, pointing out this was her area of expertise. His request had filled her with pride and pleasure, yet in spite of his praise and satisfaction she remained convinced that there was something wrong between them.

There was a distance, a reserve in Jaul that had not been there before, and he had not made love to her since their wedding night. Of course, he had been forced to sit up late with his visitors, she acknowledged ruefully.

He had come to bed in the early hours and had still risen at the crack of dawn as he always did. But since that first night, he hadn't touched her at all, indeed had suddenly become very restrained in his behaviour in a way that was totally unfamiliar and confusing to Chrissie because Jaul was such a naturally physical person. Last night, for instance, she had shifted over to his side of the bed and he had lain there as rigid as an icicle being threatened by the heat of a fire. Chrissie had intended to make encouraging moves herself but the polite goodnight he had murmured had made her pull back from that idea.

Maybe, she thought anxiously, now that she was available all the time, as it were, she didn't have quite the same appeal. Or more probably, common sense suggested gently, he was simply exhausted by early starts, late nights and the need for constant courteous diplomacy while he worked with the different factions involved in the talks that were lasting, on average, eighteen hours a day. The very last thing she should be doing with Jaul, she told herself urgently, was allowing her imagination or her insecurities to conjure up seeming problems in what was probably perfectly ordinary behaviour. Their marriage was working, wasn't it? She thought it was working but the renewed closeness she had fancied she saw during their second wedding night seemed to have evaporated again.

When they arrived back at the palace, Bandar greeted them in the entrance porch to speak urgently to Jaul. Jaul pokered up and a flush mantled his exotic cheekbones, his response to his aide clipped and cool in tone.

'What's happened?' Chrissie asked worriedly.

A tiny muscle pulled tight at the corner of Jaul's unsmiling mouth. 'My grandmother has arrived in Marwan and has asked to see me. She's staying at an hotel in the city.'

'My goodness, she must be quite an age now,' Chrissie remarked.

'I understand that she is travelling with her daughter, Rose. Obviously at some stage she remarried…my grandfather did not,' Jaul could not resist reminding her.

'I suppose, taking into account how he and your father felt about her, it would be an awkward and uncomfortable meeting for you *but*—'

Jaul froze and fell still.' I have no intention of agreeing to a meeting with the ladies. I have instructed Bandar to send my apologies and an appropriate gift.'

Chrissie closed a dismayed hand over his arm and tugged him into one of the many cluttered reception rooms off the ground-floor hall of the palace. 'You *can't* mean that?'

Jaul frowned down at her, his stunning bone structure rigid. 'Please try to understand, Chrissie. I have never heard any good of Lady Sophie, only that she is a terrible troublemaker and I have quite enough to deal with at the moment without encouraging that sort of personality into my life.'

Chrissie was disconcerted by the force and strength of his comprehensive rejection of his grandmother and his aunt and had to resist an urge to risk changing the subject by asking him what else he was struggling to deal with that was so onerous that he could not spare an elderly woman a fifteen-minute hearing even when she had come so far to see him.

'You have to change your mind about this, Jaul.'

'Although I have every respect for your opinion, I

will stand firm on this,' Jaul grated, temper licking along the edges of his roughened voice. 'This is not your business.'

'Lady Sophie is the twins' great-grandmother and that makes her my business as well.'

Jaul shot her an impatient glittering golden glance and compressed his wide, shapely mouth as he took an impatient step closer to the door. 'I refuse to discuss this any further. I have told you how I feel *and* why.'

'I'll go and see her in your stead.'

Jaul swung back lightning fast from the exit he had been making. 'No, you will not. I forbid it.'

'You forbid it?' Chrissie repeated in an almost whispered undertone, wondering when and where her husband had developed the belief that he had the right to forbid her from doing anything.

'Yes, I do,' Jaul repeated grittily and he strode off.

Forbid away, my love, Chrissie thought ruefully, *I'm afraid it won't get you anywhere because it is no longer the sixteenth century when wives blindly obeyed husbandly dictates.* As far as she was concerned, good manners alone demanded that Jaul meet with the two women when they had flown out to Marwan purely on his behalf. On the other hand she could quite understand his attitude when both his grandfather and his father had made his grandmother out to be such a horrible person. Before she could lose her nerve, however, she was determined to do what she believed was right and she asked Zaliha to track down Bandar and discover which hotel Jaul's grandmother was staying in.

A couple of hours later, a well-dressed middle-aged woman introduced herself as Rose to Chrissie at the door of the hotel suite and thanked her warmly for coming in Jaul's place. 'As I said when you phoned, my mother is becoming increasingly frail and your willingness to meet her lifted her spirits.'

'But I don't know if I can do anything to break the family stalemate,' Chrissie warned the older woman ruefully.

'When my mother read about your marriage to Jaul in the newspaper, there was no stopping her,' Rose confided. 'She was convinced that her grandson's marriage to a British woman would make a difference to her grandson's attitude.'

A tiny old lady with a fluff of white hair and faded blue eyes sat in a high-backed armchair with a cane clasped between her gnarled hands. 'I'm Sophie, your husband's grandmother,' she said simply.

Chrissie stretched out her hand. 'I'm Chrissie.'

'How much have you been told about me?'

'The barest facts,' Chrissie admitted. 'Perhaps I should share my experience with Jaul's family with you.'

Tea was served while Chrissie confided her own story, feeling that it was better to be honest and admit the difficulties she had had with Sophie's late son, Lut.

At the end of Chrissie's account, Sophie sighed. 'It's a sad thing to accept that even had I got to know my son as an adult I don't think I would've liked him. Your husband's grandfather Tarif twisted Lut against me. There was never any hope of my son listening to my side of the story. Indeed Lut accused me of being a liar but I am *not* a liar. I married Tarif when I was nineteen.'

'You were only a teenager?' Chrissie gasped, suddenly comprehending the outlandish décor of the London mansion. It had been furnished by a teenager working with an unlimited budget.

The old lady smiled. 'Yes, but I considered myself to be very mature. What teenager does not? My family was very much against the marriage but I was head over heels in love and Tarif seemed so westernised and liberal. He swore that I would be his only wife and I believed that I had nothing else to worry about. Unfortunately, excellent English and European dress aren't a sufficient guide to a man's character.'

Chrissie simply listened.

'I was already pregnant by the time we returned from our honeymoon to Marwan.' Lady Sophie paused, her thoughts clearly back in the distant past. 'That's when everything changed. My husband suddenly became unavailable and we no longer shared a bedroom...'

'Had you had an argument?'

'No. I found out that my husband had a harem full of concubines.'

Chrissie's eyes flew wide in shock. *Concubines?*

'Tarif saw no reason why he should give up the lifestyle of his ancestors,' the old lady told her quietly. 'He could not understand why I could not accept his having other women because I was his wife and his queen and soon to deliver the royal heir. He considered my status the greatest honour and believed I should be content with it.'

'Good grief,' Chrissie mumbled with stricken sympathy, barely able to imagine the distress that nineteen-year-old girl must have endured when she found herself living alone and unsupported in such a situation. 'What did you do?'

'I begged him to give his other women up and he refused. He was a very stubborn man. For months we shared the same wing of the palace while living as strangers. I gave birth to Lut. Afterwards, Tarif urged me to accept him as he was. He argued that it was enough of a sacrifice that he had promised not to take another wife.' Jaul's grandmother pursed her lips. 'Naturally I said no. A few weeks later my father died very suddenly and I flew home for the funeral. Tarif refused to let me take Lut with me. While I was away he phoned me and told me not to return to Marwan unless I had changed my mind about what I was willing to live with.'

'Obviously you never had a choice,' Chrissie commented quietly. 'That was cruel.'

'When I wouldn't give way and return to Marwan on his terms, Tarif refused to let me see my son. I didn't see Lut again until he was in his twenties and although he let me tell him my story, he wouldn't accept it. Lut was an enormous prude. The very word *concubine* set him off in a rage and he harangued me, accusing me of telling foul lies to besmirch his father's memory.'

Chrissie sighed. 'I'll discuss this with Jaul. He's not remotely like his father.'

'Are you absolutely sure of that?' Lady Sophie prompted with a worried look on her face. 'I can tell you that in terms of looks, Jaul is the living image of his grandfather and such sensitive issues as concubines are not discussed here where the King is omnipotent.'

Chrissie thanked her hostess for the tea before she departed with her thoughts in turmoil. She was convinced by the old lady's story, she acknowledged uneasily. But how did she know for sure that there were no longer concubines in the vastness of the royal palace complex? Was it even possible that she herself should need to fear such a situation? Could Jaul have honed his superb talents in the bedroom with nameless women in some hidden, never-discussed harem? Could it even provide an explanation for his marked lack of interest in making love to his wife? Or was she being insane in nourishing such a fantastic suspicion?

The question that she was determined not to ask Jaul grew and grew on the drive back to the palace. How likely was it that Jaul kept concubines like his not so very westernised grandfather? In this day and age not very likely, her rational mind assured her as she mounted the stairs to their private wing and went straight to see the twins.

Thirty minutes later, she glanced up to see Jaul lodged in the doorway, stunning eyes dark as coal and steady in the taut lines of his lean, darkly handsome face as he studied her.

'You know where I've been.' Chrissie sighed as she scrambled upright to follow Jaul into the room next door.

'You went against my wishes. Naturally I am annoyed,' Jaul spelled out flatly, his perfect white teeth grinding together with the strain of suppressing his temper as he stared down at her.

Of course he didn't want his wife connecting with a bitter old woman he had heard described as a fantasist! Of course he didn't want his grandmother trying to poison Chrissie with her undying hatred of his family! Chrissie already had all too many reasons to think badly of him. Furthermore, with his long-awaited meeting with Yusuf due to take place that very afternoon, Jaul was ready to confront the last of the devils that had haunted him since his receipt of Yusuf's note of apology, but quite understandably on edge at the prospect. Only when he was convinced that he knew *everything* could he talk honestly to Chrissie. There would be no more secrets between them, no unanswered questions or doubts. His wife deserved that from him at the very least.

'I visited Sophie because I hoped that in some way… goodness knows how…I might be able to heal the family rift,' Chrissie told him ruefully.

'A compassionate thought,' Jaul conceded grittily. 'What did she tell you about my family?'

Chrissie breathed in deep, mustering her courage. 'That your grandfather had concubines while he was married to her.'

Jaul looked at her in wonderment. 'She told you… *that*? *Seriously?*'

Chagrined by his patent disbelief, Chrissie murmured quietly, 'And I believed her.'

Jaul threw back his broad shoulders, his anger as instant and shattering as a sudden clap of thunder on a hot, humid day. 'That's a most offensive untruth…an outrageous calumny!'

'Is it?' Chrissie almost whispered because the atmosphere was so explosive it was as if all the oxygen were being sucked into a void. 'Because, naturally, after being told that I have to ask you if *you*—'

'Don't you *dare* ask that of me!' Jaul roared back at her, shocking her into sudden silence. Outright fury had charged his lean, hard-muscled frame. His dark eyes were blazing like golden arrows aimed at a target.

Chrissie had lost colour. She hadn't even got the actual question voiced but he knew exactly what she had been about to ask him and he was outraged to a degree that went beyond anything she had ever seen in him before.

'You have just proved my father's contention that his mother was an appalling liar.'

'If that is true, possibly he inherited that talent from his mother,' Chrissie challenged without hesitation. 'Your father was no great fan of the truth himself.'

Jaul paled beneath his bronzed skin and his hands closed into tight fists, for he could not defend his late father and he would not lie in his defence either. His father had been an irredeemable liar and in that moment he could quite understand why Chrissie had refused to accept Lut's view of Lady Sophie and had preferred to make up her own mind.

'There have not been concubines in the palace for over a century,' Jaul informed her curtly. 'To suggest that that lifestyle was still in existence in the nineteen thirties is incredible, but if it makes you feel any happier I will check those facts with Yusuf this afternoon. In Marwan, he is still the acknowledged authority on the history of the royal family. Indeed, he wrote a much-admired book on the subject.'

'Don't place your faith in the belief that your grandmother is lying,' Chrissie urged ruefully, thinking that very occasionally her husband could be startlingly naive. 'The book was probably a whitewash sanctioned and proofread by your father, Jaul. I bet there's not a disrespectful, critical word in it.'

As the exact same thought had already occurred to Jaul, he swallowed hard, black lashes lowering over his lustrous golden eyes. 'You are undoubtedly right but Yusuf will tell me the truth on all counts,' he declared with assurance. 'But nothing can ever eradicate the effect of my wife actually asking me if I too have kept concubines.'

Chrissie flushed a slow, painful pink. 'I didn't ask—'

'But you were dying to ask,' Jaul cut in drily. 'Do you trust me so little still? Do you really believe that my people would accept a man leading a dissolute life on their throne? My country wants to be seen as modern and forward-thinking and our women have an increasingly strong voice in society. I must be seen to practise what I preach in public *and* in private...'

What Jaul said was common sense and Chrissie was mortified that for a few overwrought minutes after leaving his grandmother's presence she had entertained such fantastic suspicions. Even more crucially she had not missed the flash of pain in his eyes that she could even think to ask him such a question. He was furious too but thankfully not in the same way as his late father. He didn't suffer from uncontrollable rages and watched his tongue when he lost his temper but the downside of those positives was that he would be pretty much silent until he had mulled everything over in depth.

'I'm sorry!' Chrissie said loudly and abruptly as he began to turn away. 'It was stupid...but just for a moment I felt I had to know for sure,' she endeavoured to explain, struck to the heart by his condemnation but not sure she could blame him for it.

'If you appreciated how prim and proper my father was you would never have felt that need,' Jaul asserted with a wry curve of his sensual mouth. 'He waged a war against immorality in every form inside and outside the palace. He was a repressive ruler. One of my first acts was to repeal the law restricting music and dancing in public places. If it makes you feel any happier about things, I will ask Yusuf to fill me in on what he knows about my father's dealings with my grandmother.'

As Jaul left the room with the giving of that concession, Chrissie slumped down on a sofa. Maybe she shouldn't have interfered by visiting Lady Sophie, she reasoned heavily. She had waded in blindly, seeing herself as doing something good and helpful but in actuality she had hurt and offended Jaul. His self-control in the face of the provocation she had offered could only embarrass her because she had controlled neither her imagination nor her tongue. In the circumstances Jaul had been very understanding and that shamed her the most. He was never going to love a woman stupid enough to ask him if he kept concubines, was he?

Jaul spent a couple of hours talking to his father's former aide. Yusuf left, relieved to have cleared his conscience of the secrets he had kept throughout his working career. Jaul, however, was in a far less happy frame of mind. In point of fact, he was stunned, furious and bitter and as soon as the keys he had requested were brought to him he strode through the huge palace complex and down a flight of stairs in a far corner. A servant wrestled with the giant key and then Jaul waved his guards back and entered the building alone.

The sheer size of the place shook Jaul even more. He prowled through empty rooms and courtyards, studied fountains and bathing places. Everything was in very good condition and he marvelled that his father's mania for historic conservation had triumphed over the older man's desire to rewrite the past and bury the family's murkier secrets. Rage was his overriding response to what he had learned from Yusuf until the point when he focused on the great bed placed on a dais. Slowly his dark, angry eyes widened as he finally registered the tenor of the murals swirling across the walls round the bed.

Utterly disconcerted, he froze, imagining his strait-laced father's reaction to such artistic licence and something infinitely more surprising bubbled up inside Jaul without warning. Gales of incredulous laughter convulsed his lean, powerful frame and when he had recovered from his inappropriate amusement he lounged back breathless against the edge of the bed. His brilliant eyes flared to the purest gold when he pictured how Chrissie would react to the paintings.

A note was delivered to Chrissie minutes after she had emerged from a long relaxing bath. Instantly recognising Jaul's copperplate black print, she tore it open.

You are cordially invited to spend a night in the harem with your husband.

A surprised giggle fell from her lips while a warm sense of relief swelled inside her. Jaul had recovered sufficiently from his annoyance with her to make a joke. It was a joke, of course it was, and Jaul had always had a terrific sense of humour. She leafed through drawers and selected her fanciest lingerie with hot cheeks before choosing a perfectly circumspect plain blue tailored dress, which gave not the smallest hint of what she wore underneath. A night in the harem? What did that entail? Her entire skin surface heated up and she smiled dreamily, knowing exactly what she was hoping that note meant while being wryly amused by her own secret conviction that there was something different about Jaul in recent days. Didn't that note prove how mistaken she had been?

One of Jaul's guards was waiting to take her to her husband and they trudged a long way down endless corridors and down stone flights of stairs before they reached their destination. A big, ugly, ironclad door faced them. Opening it for her, the guard stood back and Chrissie entered, wondering why the man was trying not to smile. But that question was quickly answered because a spectacular scene confronted her two steps beyond the door.

Candles were burning everywhere she looked, glowing in the dark to cast leaping shadows across the soaring domed ceiling and elaborate mosaic-tiled walls and ensuring that the water droplets cascading from the fountains sparkled like diamonds. It was beautiful, incredibly beautiful, and Chrissie knew instinctively that Jaul had done it for her. Her bright eyes stung painfully and she had to blink when the man himself appeared from behind a pillar about thirty feet from her. In contrast to their highly exotic surroundings Jaul sported faded jeans and a partially unbuttoned white shirt, the pale fabric accentuating his bronzed skin and the blackness of his unruly hair. For a split second she felt as though time itself had slipped for this was Jaul as she remembered him as a student, shorn of every atom of his forbidding reserve.

'Where on earth are we?' Chrissie asked.

'In the heart of the al-Zahid family's shadiest secret,' Jaul proffered wryly. 'The harem that even I didn't know still existed until this evening. Of course, I knew there would have been one at some stage but, taking into account my father's delicate sensibilities, I assumed it was long gone.'

Chrissie gazed past him at the giant bed. 'That looks like a bed people would throw an orgy on,' she said before she could think better of it. 'Not that I know anything about…er…orgies—'

'Look at the walls,' Jaul invited.

In the flickering shadows she saw the murals and the naked male and female figures engaged in flagrant sexual play and a hot flush lit her cheeks. 'My goodness…'

'I'm amazed that my father didn't have this place razed to the ground, but he idolised my grandfather.' Jaul sighed. 'How he retained that respectful attitude when confronted with the reality that Tarif was a man with licentious habits, I cannot begin to imagine.'

'Nor can I,' she whispered, beginning to understand why he had brought her to the harem. He had found out the truth and immediately acted with the open-minded candour she had always loved him for. When Jaul was in the wrong he never tried to cover it up or excuse himself.

'I've phoned Sophie's daughter, Rose, and apologised through her for taking so long to make an approach to my grandmother.'

'You phoned Rose…*already*?' Chrissie exclaimed.

'There were concubines here well into the last century. My grandmother *wasn't* lying,' Jaul confirmed with a sardonic twist of his lips. 'But I only learned the truth this afternoon from Yusuf. He knows all the family secrets and learning about how cruelly my grandmother was treated was only the first of several shocks I received after I questioned him.'

A frown dividing her brows, Chrissie made an instinctive move forward and rested her hand soothingly on his forearm, feeling the muscles that were pulled whipcord tight with fierce tension. 'I'm sorry, Jaul.'

As if he found her touch unbearable, Jaul shifted back a defensive step. 'For what are you sorry? That I was too much of a fool to appreciate that my father would say or do anything to *wreck* my marriage?' he framed with unleashed bitterness. 'Chrissie, I would've trusted him with my life! He was a difficult man and very controlling but in many of the ways that mattered he *was* a good father.'

Discomfited by his rejection of her sympathy, Chrissie stiffened. 'And you loved him, *of course* you did. I loved my mother when I was a child even though I had a pretty miserable childhood. Parents don't have to be perfect to be loved. But I still don't understand why your father stayed so dead set against his own mother and me when he knew your grandfather was the one at fault.'

'My father chose the easy way out. He was never going to admit the embarrassing truth. If he laid the blame of cultural differences at his mother's door, he could continue to idolise his father and believe that he was right to protect me from all Western influences.' Jaul's brilliant dark eyes veiled. 'Apparently he was afraid that I may have inherited Tarif's fatal weakness for women. I was finally able to understand why I had to rebel against him to gain the right to study in the UK.'

Chrissie was listening closely. 'You had to...*rebel*? You never told me that before.'

'I was ashamed of it. I was raised to believe that a decent son always respects a parent's greater maturity and wisdom,' Jaul admitted grudgingly. 'After the experience of a military boarding school followed by army life, I longed for the freedom to make my own choices.'

'Of course you did,' she whispered feelingly, newly aware of what a domineering old tyrant his late father had been. 'And I respect you more for having taken a stand and it's hardly surprising that you went a little wild when you first started university. I never appreciated how restricted your life had been before you came to the UK.'

Jaul studied her lovely face fixedly, the turquoise eyes soft with compassion. He was shaken that she was still trying to comfort him when he didn't deserve comfort because he had let her down worst of all. 'But that period of going wild almost cost me you,' he pointed out. 'It gave you the wrong impression.'

Tears stung her eyes and she blinked them back in desperation as she sat down on the flat tiled edge of a fountain. 'There was no way I was going to resist you for ever…the attraction was too strong.'

'I have never wanted any woman as much as I wanted you,' Jaul admitted in a raw undertone and he bent over the tray stationed on a table by a pillar to fill a glass and extend it to her. 'I have never loved any woman but you…'

At that statement, her hand shook a little as she accepted the glass, hastily sipping the cool sweetness of fruit juice. He had never loved anyone else, she was thinking, that surely had to be a point in her favour.

His lean, darkly handsome features were grim and taut with tension. In a restive, uncertain gesture he raked long, elegant fingers through his luxuriant hair, tousling it. 'I loved you yet I let you down. You were alone and pregnant and I wasn't with you. I accepted my father's lies.'

Chrissie's heart was thumping very hard. 'Jaul— what's brought all this on tonight?'

'Yusuf was with my father when he visited you in Oxford. His conscience was uneasy and he was eager to clear it,' Jaul recounted flatly. 'I was appalled when Yusuf described what happened that day. It shames me that my father could have treated my wife in such a way and that I was unable to prevent it from happening.'

The backs of her eyes were gritty with tears because she was remembering what had been one of the worst days of her life. Confronted by King Lut, she had felt alone and helpless, not to mention devastated by her father-in-law's complete rejection of her as his son's wife. 'You were in hospital,' she reminded him shakily. 'There was nothing you could have done.'

'Yusuf told me the truth.' Jaul was ashen below his dark skin, his brilliant eyes tortured as he gazed at her. 'But let us be honest here—Yusuf told me truths which I should've accepted when *you* spoke them.'

'Yes,' Chrissie cut in to confirm without hesitation. 'I have never lied to you…' A split second of silence fell before she coloured and added, 'Well, only once and I'll sort that out later.'

'I swallowed my father's lies about you and in my bitterness and hurt I learned to distrust my every memory of you. When I came back to find you last month, I should have *listened* more, thought deeper.'

'Naturally you trusted your father's word when he told you that I'd taken the money and run.'

'How was it natural?' His tone derisive in emphasis, Jaul set down her glass with a definite crack. Dark eyes flaming gold, he studied her, nostrils flaring, beautiful stubborn mouth tight at the corners with strain. 'You were my life. You were my wife. My first loyalty should always have been to you. Will you please stop trying to make excuses for my failure to support you when you *most* needed me?' he demanded hoarsely. 'I let you down in every way possible—'

'Your father did this to us. He separated us, lied to us both and hurt us both,' Chrissie responded shakily. 'Put the blame where it belongs, Jaul. You were in a coma and then you had surgery and were struggling to recuperate. You weren't in any condition to fight my corner or yours. When your father lied to you then, you were very vulnerable—'

'I'm trying to say sorry, trying to grovel but you won't let me,' Jaul muttered unevenly, his eyes suspiciously bright.

'I don't want you grovelling. I don't want your guilt—'

'This is not guilt, this is...*shame*,' he labelled roughly. 'You are my wife and I let you down and I don't want to lose you. There's nothing I won't do or say to keep you as my wife!'

Recognising his increasingly emotional frame of mind, Chrissie almost smiled. 'Oh, I think I worked that out straight after that pre-nuptial agreement was stuffed beneath my nose when I looked as though I might be ready to walk away from you,' she confided.

'It was an empty threat,' Jaul confessed grittily. 'A pre-nup has no standing as yet in a British court of law. In addition you signed it without the benefit of independent legal advice and you were very young at the time. I knew that the pre-nup wasn't worth the paper it was written on.'

It was Chrissie's turn to be taken aback. As she had listened her eyes had widened and her soft mouth had hardened. 'I should've called your bluff. But maybe I didn't fight more because I didn't want to. Has that occurred to you?'

His lush black lashes swept up and down over his frowning eyes. 'But why would you have behaved that way?'

Chrissie stiffened, reluctant to give him the words of love that were as effective as chains in binding her to both him and the twins. He knew the truth now about his father, her pride and her sense of justice finally satisfied. He knew what she had endured and he knew that she had not accepted a financial settlement in lieu of their supposedly invalid marriage. Keen to change the subject of why she was being so tolerant of his stubborn misjudgements, she said with forced lightness of tone, 'Who on earth lit all these candles?'

'Zaliha supplied the candles and the snacks. I lit them. The fountains have been kept in good working order and only had to be switched on. I couldn't allow any other female staff in here because they would have been very much shocked by the murals.'

Chrissie scanned the hundreds of candles and hid a smile, touched by the effort he had made on her behalf. 'The murals may be shocking but this place is beautiful all lit up like this.'

The beginnings of the smile that had relaxed her full pink mouth filled Jaul with a craving for the softness of her, the warmth and the strength that ran like a core of inner steel through her seemingly fragile body. He had never appreciated how strong she truly was until he'd learnt what she had had to withstand at his father's hands. His lean brown hands snapped into fists, anger stirring afresh because he had been incapable of protecting her. The guilt, which he was struggling to master, felt insurmountable.

'I should've contacted you as soon as I was mobile again,' he stated with savage regret, the hard, sculpted planes of his darkly handsome face stark with strain in the flickering light. 'But I couldn't face seeing you again knowing that I had lost you... It is hard for me to admit that but it is, at least, the truth of my feelings back then. Seeing you again, being in your presence when you were no longer mine, would have hurt too much.'

'It still mattered that much to you?' Chrissie pressed in surprise.

Jaul shot her an incredulous look. 'I loved you. I loved you with all my heart! But I lost faith in you while I lay alone in hospital.'

Pained regret slivered through Chrissie. She was furious that his father had subjected him to that ordeal of believing that she no longer cared about him. *I loved you with all my heart.* It hurt Chrissie to hear that. 'I would've been there with you if I'd known—'

'I know that now...that's what killing me!' he bit out, swinging defensively away from her, broad shoulders bunched with tension below his thin shirt.

'But it's pointless wasting all this energy on a past that's gone, done and dusted,' she declared, tilting her chin. 'We have to move on from it—'

'How can I do that when my father's lies cost us so much?' Jaul framed emotively, turning back to her. 'Once you were mine, completely, utterly mine and it is my dream that some day you will feel like that again. But, sensible and fair as I have tried to be, I still find myself thinking wholly unjust thoughts about the fact that—' His hands fisted again and he turned away again. 'No, I won't say it…such jealousy and possessiveness are wrong!'

Chrissie was frowning. 'What the heck are you talking about?' she prompted uncertainly.

'It is a topic better not discussed. What has happened has happened and we will not allow it to spoil what we do have,' Jaul declared, still restively pacing the tiled floor.

Jealousy? Possessiveness? Abruptly she grasped his meaning and she reddened, cheeks heating fierily. 'Are you talking about the fact that I said I was with other men while we were apart?'

His lustrous gaze narrowed. 'It's not something we need to discuss,' he told her hastily. 'You believed you were single and quite naturally…'

'Well, maybe it would've been natural but I didn't sleep with anyone else,' Chrissie told him in a rush. 'I said I did but it was a lie. I don't know how you thought I could have found the time for another man when I was pregnant most of the first year you were gone and saddled with two newborns and working the second year.'

Jaul was studying her with fixed attention. 'You… *lied*?' he queried in disbelief. 'About such an important issue?'

Chrissie winced. 'It was a weapon and I used it. It's the one and only lie I have told you. Obviously I assumed that *you*—'

Jaul stalked closer and gripped her forearms to hold

her still. '*No*. No concubines, no girlfriends, no one-night stands. Nothing…zilch.'

Her eyes opened very wide in surprise. 'But…er, why?'

'When I finally got out of that wheelchair I decided that since I had got myself in such a mess with you it would be safer to avoid another liaison and instead get married.'

The tension in Chrissie's slight shoulders relaxed and then reached full strength again because, while she was relieved he had not had any other women and his clear gaze convinced her that the once bitten, twice shy adage had worked a blinder on him, she still wanted to know who he had planned to marry. 'So, who was picked to replace me?'

Jaul flushed. 'I didn't have anyone picked but I knew my people were waiting for me to do the picking.' He brushed a gentle finger beneath her down-curved chin to raise it. 'In truth, Chrissie, I have never cared for any woman the way I care for you. I don't deserve you but you have always owned my heart—from the first moment to the last moment. I was depressed for a long time after I believed I had lost you and I was afraid of ever feeling for another woman what I felt for you.'

She lifted her hands to frame his proud cheekbones with tender fingers, emotion bright in her eyes as she gazed up into the scorching heat of his. 'And I'm afraid that I'm always going to love you,' she told him rue-fully. 'When you first came back I honestly did think I hated you but I never did get over losing you either.'

'Chrissie—'

'Shush,' she hushed him tenderly. 'Nobody else compared, nobody else can make me *feel* what you do and I do believe that you love me too.'

'I do. I love you very deeply, *habibti*.' Jaul planted a kiss against her caressing fingers, his black lashes low over golden eyes shimmering with a happiness Chrissie could not mistake. 'The day I threatened you with the pre-nup was the day I understood that I still loved you because I have never done anything so dishonest in my whole life. And I wasn't even ashamed. There was literally nothing I wouldn't do to get a second chance with you and our children.'

Chrissie wrapped her arms round his neck. 'Ruthlessness in pursuit of the right goal is acceptable.'

All her tension evaporated while he held her close and heat of a different ilk warmed at her feminine core.

'But…who is to say…what the right goal is?' Jaul quipped, running down the zip on her dress to ease it off her shoulders.

As the dress dropped to her feet, exposing the frilly silky lingerie he loved to see her in, he made a sound of appreciation low in his throat and carried her over to the orgy-sized bed to settle her down on the white linen sheet.

'My only goal,' he proffered softly, 'is to keep you as my wife and the mother of my children for ever and make you so happy that you eventually forget our separation.'

Chrissie plucked at his collar. 'I think that's a terrific motivation,' she told him sassily, her bright eyes dancing as he ripped off his shirt with more haste than cool. 'Particularly since you've been so very separate from me in bed this past week…and I haven't been at all happy.'

Jaul dealt her a troubled glance. 'I burned for you but once I received Yusuf's note...'

'What note?'

Jaul explained the note. 'And in the same moment I read it I knew I had got everything wrong with you. I couldn't afford to take anything for granted.'

His wife ran worshipping fingers idly along the rippling muscles of his abdomen. 'I thought you'd lost interest.'

'You must be joking!' Jaul exclaimed, rolling her back to come down over her, his taut lower body hard with an arousal she could feel. 'I always want you. I just knew I didn't deserve you.'

Chrissie ran an appreciative hand down over a lean, powerful thigh. 'Love makes people more forgiving and I love you an awful lot.'

His kiss was hot, hungry and wildly exciting and her heart pounded and her pulses raced. Happiness was spinning and dancing inside her like a sudden burst of golden sunshine.

'And I love you,' he confessed with a flashing grin that tugged at her heart because the twins so strongly resembled him. 'I love you more than I ever thought I could love anyone and I always will.'

Three years after that incredibly romantic reconciliation in the former harem, Chrissie watched the twins squabble over a ride-on plastic car they were playing with in a shaded courtyard. At four years old, Tarif and Soraya were lively and opinionated and in need of firm handling from both their parents. Rising, Chrissie uttered a sharp word to break up the quarrel, threatening to remove the car entirely if the children refused to share it peaceably. It was interesting to sit back down again and watch her children negotiate a compromise.

Lizzie phoned while Chrissie was savouring peppermint tea served with tiny cakes. Smoothing the barely visible bump that thickened her figure, she thought how grateful she was that her morning sickness had not lasted into her second trimester. Indeed her second pregnancy was progressing much more smoothly than her first and she put that down to the lack of stress in her current life. She chatted at length to her sister, who was due to arrive with her family and their father for a visit at the end of the week. Her family were regular visitors and distance had not driven a wedge between the sisters.

When their nanny reclaimed the twins for an early evening meal, Chrissie wandered down to the stables to visit Hero. Two years earlier, her elderly pony had arrived to take up residence in the ritziest stall in the royal block. Their reunion had been a wonderful surprise for Chrissie and she had been overwhelmed that Jaul, incredibly busy as he was, had taken the time and trouble to ensure that Hero could live out what remained of his days near his mistress in Marwan.

Having become heavily involved in the development of the nursery education programme, Chrissie had found her first year in Marwan had raced past her. Jaul's people were friendly and supportive and although she sometimes attended formal occasions with Jaul, rubbing shoulders with diplomats, foreign dignitaries and businessmen, for much of the time she was simply Jaul's wife. Family life and time to spend with the children were immensely important to both of them.

Having visited Hero, Chrissie headed back to their

private wing to shower and change. Every year they celebrated that night the barriers between them had finally dropped and they spent the night in the harem. That was where they had rediscovered their love and happiness and it was a wonderful way of remembering how they had started out and keeping faith with the promises they had exchanged.

Dusk was falling when Jaul began lighting candles and a meal was being set out below the pillars. The murals were covered by discreet curtains, ensuring that no staff member could be shocked or offended by those depictions of earthly lust and love. Jaul liked to think that love must have featured in some of the relationships that had taken place in the harem but he could not begin to imagine how his grandfather Tarif had chosen shallow physical relationships over the far deeper and more lasting bonds he could have formed with the wife who had loved him.

Jaul frowned as he thought of his grandmother, regretting that their time together had been so short. Lady Sophie had died peacefully in her sleep the year before. Prior to that, Jaul had made frequent visits to the old lady's home in London, keen to make up as best he could for the decades his late father had spent ignoring his mother's very existence.

The iron ring on the huge outer door was smartly rapped and rapped a second time when he was only halfway down the room to answer it. Jaul grinned, well acquainted with his wife's impatience.

'I haven't quite finished the candles,' he warned her.

'I'm here to help.' Chrissie looked up into his stunning dark golden eyes and could have sworn that her knees wobbled.

'No, you're pregnant. You're not allowed to do anything but put your feet up.' Jaul ushered her over to an armchair furnished with a footstool.

'Anything?' Chrissie teased as she kicked off her shoes and sat down.

'Conserve your energy for what's really important.' Glancing wickedly at the bed awaiting them with his eyes alight with amusement, Jaul knelt down beside her to reach for her hand and slide a platinum ring adorned with a glowing sapphire onto her middle finger. 'Thank you for another wonderful year.'

Chrissie studied her latest gift in consternation. 'We agreed that you weren't going to buy me any more jewellery.'

'I didn't agree. I simply chose silence over argument.'

'Sometimes you can be so devious.' Chrissie lifted a hand to brush an errant lock of blue-black hair off his brow.

'And you love it,' Jaul told her with assurance, planting a kiss on the delicate skin of her inner wrist while tracing tender fingertips over the slight swell of her pregnant tummy. 'You wear everything you feel on the surface but I hide it…except when I'm with you. I love you, *habibti.*'

'I know.' And Chrissie gloried in that sense of security, standing up to enable him to band his arms around her and claim her mouth with the hunger that neither of them ever tried to hide or suppress.

'I'm so excited about the baby,' he confided. 'I missed so much with the twins. This time around I will treasure every moment with you.'

'I bet you embarrass me by fainting or something,' Chrissie forecast, surveying him with loving intensity as the dancing light and shadow of the candles played over his lean, strong face.

But Jaul won that bet. He was fully conscious for the birth of his second son, Prince Hafiz, a healthy seven-pound baby with his mother's astonishingly blue eyes. There was a hint of his English grandfather in his bone structure. His elder brother gave him a teddy and Soraya gave him a picture she had drawn. In the first official photographs, with Hafiz's parents holding him safe in their arms, happiness and contentment radiated from the entire royal family.

* * * * *

#3341 SHEIKH'S FORBIDDEN CONQUEST
The Howard Sisters
by Chantelle Shaw

Sultan Kadir Al Sulaimar's first duty must be to his country, but feisty helicopter pilot Lexi Howard's disregard for his command is somewhat...refreshing. Can the desert king resist making her his final—and most forbidden—conquest before his arranged marriage?

#3342 TEMPTED BY HER BILLIONAIRE BOSS
The Tenacious Tycoons
by Jennifer Hayward

Harrison Grant can't afford distractions with a high-stakes deal on the table, but his new assistant, Francesca Masseria, is a beautiful diversion. And what he's beginning to want from Francesca isn't part of her job description!

#3343 SEDUCED INTO THE GREEK'S WORLD
by Dani Collins

For Natalie Adams, an affair in Paris with billionaire Demitri Makricosta surpasses her *wildest* dreams! But the closer Natalie gets to emotions he's locked away, the more Demitri tries to distract her to ensure that seduction remains the *only* thing between them...

#3344 MARRIED FOR THE PRINCE'S CONVENIENCE
by Maya Blake

Jasmine Nichols is catapulted to the top of the prospective brides list when Prince Reyes discovers she's carrying his heir! Except Reyes's cold, tactical marriage is about to be jeopardized by their explosive chemistry and what he learns when he uncovers his new bride's secrets...

REQUEST YOUR FREE BOOKS!

HARLEQUIN

Presents®

2 FREE NOVELS PLUS
2 FREE GIFTS!

PASSION
GUARANTEED
SEDUCTION

YES! Please send me 2 FREE Harlequin Presents® novels and my 2 FREE gifts (gifts are worth about $10). After receiving them, if I don't wish to receive any more books, I can return the shipping statement marked "cancel." If I don't cancel, I will receive 6 brand-new novels every month and be billed just $4.30 per book in the U.S. or $5.24 per book in Canada. That's a saving of at least 13% off the cover price! It's quite a bargain! Shipping and handling is just 50¢ per book in the U.S. and 75¢ per book in Canada.* I understand that accepting the 2 free books and gifts places me under no obligation to buy anything. I can always return a shipment and cancel at any time. Even if I never buy another book, the two free books and gifts are mine to keep forever.

106/306 HDN GHRP

Name _____ (PLEASE PRINT)

Address _____ Apt. #

City _____ State/Prov. _____ Zip/Postal Code

Signature (if under 18, a parent or guardian must sign)

Mail to the **Reader Service:**
IN U.S.A.: P.O. Box 1867, Buffalo, NY 14240-1867
IN CANADA: P.O. Box 609, Fort Erie, Ontario L2A 5X3

**Are you a current subscriber to Harlequin Presents® books
and want to receive the larger-print edition?
Call 1-800-873-8635 or visit www.ReaderService.com.**

* Terms and prices subject to change without notice. Prices do not include applicable taxes. Sales tax applicable in N.Y. Canadian residents will be charged applicable taxes. Offer not valid in Quebec. This offer is limited to one order per household. Not valid for current subscribers to Harlequin Presents books. All orders subject to credit approval. Credit or debit balances in a customer's account(s) may be offset by any other outstanding balance owed by or to the customer. Please allow 4 to 6 weeks for delivery. Offer available while quantities last.

Your Privacy—The Reader Service is committed to protecting your privacy. Our Privacy Policy is available online at www.ReaderService.com or upon request from the Reader Service.

We make a portion of our mailing list available to reputable third parties that offer products we believe may interest you. If you prefer that we not exchange your name with third parties, or if you wish to clarify or modify your communication preferences, please visit us at www.ReaderService.com/consumerschoice or write to us at Reader Service Preference Service, P.O. Box 9062, Buffalo, NY 14240-9062. Include your complete name and address.

HP15

SPECIAL EXCERPT FROM

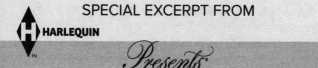

HARLEQUIN

Presents

*Maximiliano Fonseca Roselli might need his secretary,
Darcy Lennox, to help him seal the deal of the century,
but will just one scorching kiss make him realize that
the stakes are far, far higher…?*

Read on for a sneak preview of
THE BRIDE FONSECA NEEDS,
the second book in
Abby Green's
passion-filled duet
BILLIONAIRE BROTHERS.

"Look, I didn't plan to announce an engagement to you this evening."

"I'm not so sure you didn't, Max. It certainly seemed to trip off your tongue very easily—along with that very inventive plan to treat me to a Devilliers ring. Tell me, are we taking your private jet?"

He glared at her. "I didn't plan it. He just… *Dio.* You heard him."

Darcy's insides tightened as she recalled the sense of protectiveness that had arisen when Montgomery had baldly dissected Max's life. He'd remained impervious in the face of much worse provocation. *But this had been personal. About his family.*

Darcy stood up, feeling vulnerable. "I heard him, Max. The man clearly has strong feelings about the importance of family, but do you think he really cares if you're married or not?"

"He believes my perspective will be skewed unless I have

someone to worry about other than myself."

"So you fed me to him?"

He looked at her. "Yes."

"I'm just a means to an end—so you can get your hands on that fund."

Max looked at Darcy. Why did those words strike at him somewhere? Of *course* she was a means to an end. And that end was in sight.

"Yes, you *are*— I won't pretty it up and lie to you. But, Darcy, if you do this you won't walk away empty-handed. You can name your price."

She let out a short, curt laugh and it made Max wince inwardly. It sounded so unlike her.

"Believe me, no price could buy me as your wife, Max."

Max felt that like a blow to his gut, but he gritted out, "I'm not *buying* a wife, Darcy. I'm asking you to do this as part of your job. Admittedly it's a little above and beyond the call of duty…but you will be well compensated."

Darcy tossed her head. "Nothing could induce me to do this."

"Nothing…?" Max asked silkily as he moved a little closer, his vision suddenly overwhelmed with the tantalizing way Darcy filled out her dress.

She put out a hand. "Stop right there."

Max stopped, but his blood was still leaping. He'd yet to meet a woman he couldn't seduce. *Was he prepared to seduce Darcy into agreement?* His mind screamed caution, but his body screamed *yes!*

Don't miss
THE BRIDE FONSECA NEEDS by Abby Green,
available June 2015 wherever
Harlequin Presents® books and ebooks are sold.

HARLEQUIN

Presents®

Love the drama of duty vs desire and the shocking
arrival of a secret baby? Maya Blake's passionate
and powerful story is for you!

MARRIED FOR
THE PRINCE'S
CONVENIENCE

June 2015

Jasmine Nichols is catapulted to the top of the
prospective brides list when Prince Reyes discovers
she's carrying his heir! Except Reyes's cold,
tactical marriage is about to be jeopardized by
their explosive chemistry and uncovering
his new bride's secrets…